ALIENS IN WONDERLAND

Or Everything You Ever Wanted To Know About God,
But Were Afraid To Ask

by

Alpha

Order this book online at www.trafford.com
or email orders@trafford.com

Most Trafford titles are also available at major online book retailers.

Printed in Victoria, BC, Canada.

ISBN: 978-1-4269-2316-6 (sc)

ISBN: 978-1-4269-2317-3 (dj)

Library of Congress Control Number: 2009913217

*Our mission is to efficiently provide the world's finest, most comprehensive book publishing
service, enabling every author to experience success. To find out how to publish your book, your
way, and have it available worldwide, visit us online at www.trafford.com*

Trafford rev. 01/18/2010

 www.trafford.com

North America & international
toll-free: 1 888 232 4444 (USA & Canada)
phone: 250 383 6864 ♦ fax: 812 355 4082

Lovingly dedicated to:

My dear family and friends, too numerous to mention...

Be they flesh and blood friends and relatives, or spiritual.

Special thanks go out to some very important beings, who

Helped me to complete this novella in ways that I could not

Seem to help myself with. If it had not been for them, I would

Not been able to finish this story in a timely fashion

I wish you all and those you love a perfect future and can

Only hope that you will get something out of this project.

Thanks again to my sister Dawn Browning, my niece Eryn

Angela Browning, and my friends Patrick McGuire, Rene

Bullock, Dominique Laurien, Buzz Andrews, and of course,

Rael. The lion's share of my gratitude really must go to the

Inter-Galactic Federation of Free Worlds, (IFFW), because

Without them we would not even exist, or have any of this

Information. Special thanks to you too, my dear reader.

Contents

FORWARD

It is my intention for you (y'all) to understand and identify, as only a reader can, the author's perspective concerning the issues discussed during this novel. My intention is to prepare and deliver, with Gemini grace, pertinent spiritual information regarding the renewable existence of God. You will see what I mean by renewable if you read on. And, simply, what goes on in the everyday life of certain Extraterrestrial Biological Entities (E.B.E.s). I also hope to help you discern what goes on in everyday life in and around one of Earth's most celebrated fellows and his creator/father, God. I thereby hope to establish a reasonably accurate image of these and other entities.

It is also my intention to, in the very least; bridge the gaps that exist between the religions of our generation. One gap is between our present longstanding accepted knowledge of our concept of God, and our comprehensible real God. As well, a gap exists between how we are told we should interpret and demonstrate the meaning of God and how we show our faith and prove our belief in the (living) Creator (s).

In addition, I'd like to say something regarding the real and true meaning of that place called "Hell."

CHAPTER 1

The Council of Eternals and The Elixir of Life

I was sitting in my studio one evening, listening to the blades of the ceiling fan keeping a breeze, and keeping me cool, when in walked my daughter. "Daddy, where did everything all begin and who is responsible for all of creation?" Setting aside the portion of my piano piece, specifically, part of a Sonata that I call "You're Cue"; I wiped another coffee stain from my lips onto my shirt sleeve and took a deep breath. I simply stared in her eyes for a second, and swallowed a lump that I seemed to be carrying in my own throat since childhood from my unanswered pleas for answers to the same spiritual questions. I felt puffed up with pride for my little girl's constant quest for knowledge and understanding. Somehow her curiosity made it easier for me to think and communicate with her, thus feeling confident my answers would only channel the truth through to her. I had become accustomed to the interruptions in the studio and welcomed my friends and business associates into my life, but I especially enjoyed the times when my family stopped by to say…

Hello?" she said again, rather sarcastically, as if nobody was really there. Suddenly aware of her attempt to startle me from my muse, and after a last pleasing glance towards the piano keys, I harnessed my attention, which seemed noticeably distracted, but only because of the illusion that time creates... and my mind clambered over the walls of my studio, to the sliding glass doors where I could see out over the ocean beyond the city, and stopped while I stared for a second, which seemed like a thousand years. Surprised at my own relief, I began to tell her about a movie that I had made, which attempts to explain the preparation of the universe and the creation of physical life itself. Fortunately I had previously anticipated these inquiries and prepared, I say to her, an informative film, for spongy little minds like hers. One of my very favorite times of the day is here, I thought, that evening was coming to a close, and before long, darkness would be upon us, soon after the spectacular view of the sunset out over the water. My, how that had inspired me over the years, I mused, and thought back to the many days spent on Wreck Beach cheering the setting of the Sun with friends.

Hanging out with "Sweetcloud" for a while, we closed up the studio together, and then split the scene and cruised up the path that wound its way up to our house. The anticipation and excitement seemed abnormally low-key for her. She was unusually calm, cool, and collected, for a tender seven year old about to see a movie. All that togetherness suggested the seriousness of the question she had asked... ah yes, the beauty of the true seeker.

"Do you think your little brother would like to watch it with you?" I asked her, even though I figured he was still a tad bit too young for any such lesson. "Well," she decided, "methinks this is one experience I should share with him. He'll probably enjoy it even if he doesn't understand it." Maybe when they're older I'll have a better explanation prepared for them, maybe not, but for now, this will have to do.

"Well, that's what I thought too," I replied, and continued, "I've assembled this informative material and the scenes in sort of a 'broken English' style with appropriately animated scenes. I do hope it keeps your interest and you can follow it so it all makes sense. I also hope that you enjoy it. It's just as important to me that you can have fun watching it."

The audience may discover that there is some history mystery to uncover here yet. Perhaps any such secrets will be revealed yet, maybe even by my son, Sand Avatar, or my daughter, Colour, alias Sweetcloud,

Avatar. Actually, there is a small chance that some of those mysteries will never be uncovered! Quite honestly, I can't seem to shake the fear of not being able to answer or explain each and every question. Feeling like the Seeker of the 'true seekers', I think it's important, more for myself than anyone else that these mysterious secrets are revealed, at least to me anyway, and my fear alleviated. Oh well, think positively Jiva[1], and be sure Atma[2], so as not to have these uncertain feelings, for without fear and doubt, I believe anything that is kuo[3] may, and probably will, happen.

Now, kuo is now a word that I have learned recently, while reading "Help us Welcome the Extraterrestrials", or at least I think that was the title of it...it's been a long time since I've actually read the book that was written by Claude Vohrillan. The book is based on the accounts of the experiences of Claude, nicknamed "Rael," when the "Elohim" contacted him. Elohim is a phrase, or self-given name, which in their language means "those that come from the sky."

I'm truly sorry Mr. Rael, if I've misspelled your name. I've given away the book since I bought it to a very curious friend of mine. She seemed to be seeking some of the same answers that I had been looking for. I'd also like to take this opportunity to express my disappointment for not hearing from you, or at least somebody from your faithful group of followers and believers, as I did send a letter to more than one of the addresses that I found in the first book that you've written. In the letter, I was asking for permission to reprint and publish various tidbits of information from the most interesting and intriguing novel.

I found the first book of Rael's to be highly informative, brilliant, extremely valuable and necessary reading, for the truly curious seekers of the Divine...but blatantly, and, I don't know how widely, misunderstood by the general population, at least in my immediate area of Vancouver, British Columbia, Canada (according to one review I watched on a local television station). Once they discovered that a lot of Rael's followers were sexually 'liberated', although not everybody, and that certainly isn't dogma for them, that was all they needed to discover to reach an assumed position of judgment and decide that the

---

[1]   Sanskrit; "eternal living entity."

[2]   Sanskrit; "self, the individual soul."

[3]   Common intergalactic universal language, meaning "good feeling."

whole thing consisted of a bunch of sexual perverts, and therefore they should all be considered dangerous and undesirable weirdoes. Because of this incorrect and premature judgment on the part of the media, the real and true message has been overlooked. I believe that to be a serious mistake that could have its negative consequences, which is probably what they intended.

I think that it was a rare endeavor on the part of Rael to share such a personally precious experience, and I for one, am eternally glad, and was instantly grateful for his selfless and relentlessly pursued performance. I can assure you, Rael's real message is much more than a crazy sexual 'movement' or a trivial passing phase. That local station shows a lot of narrow mindedness making such a ridiculous judgment, and not only should they be embarrassed, but they have managed to overlook Rael's amazing discovery and important message.

Incidentally, Rael's original book is partially responsible for inspiring this book of mine that I am now writing, (Aliens in Wonderland), and, depending upon the response, I'm even considering writing a sequel to it, as one of the other major instigators for Aliens in Wonderland also has a second part to it, but similarly, I've not yet digested all of the information. It isn't going to be easy for me to get a hold of that information, but as I said, I'm hoping for the best, and for those of us who are interested in learning more, I will surely do my best to try and obtain all of the relevant and pertinent information. I believe, where there is a will, there is a way.

Ah yes, kuo...although this particular word isn't from the perfect language of Sanskrit, it sneaks right into your vocabulary with refreshing ease and settles itself next to "cool". We can borrow this and 29 other useful words from; I believe they called it, the common universal language. When I said they in the previous sentence I was referring to a collective group of different races of beings that has been represented by my contact. However, the Elohim have a language all their own, which is similar to the Earth languages of Greek and Hebrew, but not quite exactly the same as either of them.

I think that kuo is probably used a lot by the E.T.s and therefore, is logically a very welcome and accepted thing to say, especially with the Elohim and their distinguished company. I believe that a small common language has been created, and accepted by various groups of E.T.s in order that the numerous space races may all use it as a simple form of communication, embrace and protect it, for it indeed embodies obvious attributes and should one day soon, I hope, be just as valuable on the tongues of the too numerous to mention races of Earthlings, at least until we can agree on one common language that is more complete. In the meantime, the untold billions of us have at least something in common. Which I believe is extremely important as there are already about 70 different races of E.T.s and Aliens that we know something about, not all of which are concerned with our wellbeing. However, fortunately, those of us that are concerned greatly outnumber and militarily outclass those of "them" that would appear to be evil.

In fact, in the last 40 years, this planet Earth has been attacked several times! Surprised? You should be equally astonished to know that if it weren't for the constant and loving protection of the various groups of E.T.s that are, believe it or not, still watching over us...we, as we know us, would have long ago ceased to exist. This I know because the bad guys that attacked us had, and have in a sense, far superior weaponry compared to us Earthlings alone. We would not have stood a chance and would now be dead or enslaved by those that did not have our best interests at heart, or even in mind for that matter. So indeed we all owe a great deal of thanks for protecting our lives and the freedom of existence that we have, to the ever-present watchful eye(s) of the loving E.T.s.

On Earth we have approximately six billion people. It is entirely possible that the planet of the Elohim is where we travel to at the time of death for judgment and, according to our karma[4], are consequently either delivered from the cycle of physical birth and death, or reincarnated according to the laws of karma and dharma[5]. If it isn't entirely obvious to you by now that this journey I am speaking of we are to make after death, quite necessarily, is a spiritual journey. Now I am not in any way negating the teachings of Edgar Cayce, John Ford, or Sylvia Browne or even your own personal beliefs, perhaps based on a near death experience, what I'm suggesting is that if you are looking

---

[4]   Sanskrit; material activities, for which one incurs subsequent reaction.

[5]   Sanskrit; religious principles, one's eternal natural occupation,(i.e.,devotional service to the Lord).

for eternal physical life then you will need to get your body and soul to the planet of the Elohim.

Now way back near the beginning of the universe, the Paramatman, or Super soul, (the indwelling aspect of the Supreme Lord, the Great Spirit, that lives in our hearts and serves as a guide and a witness), divided itself into numerous various incarnations and accordingly, each incarnation of Godhead has a specific duty, and or duties to perform. Each one of course, has its own individual title as well as function. One of these particular incarnations of Godhead is to be of certain interest to us here on Earth, as He is called YamaRaja, which means Lord of death. His duty, as chief of the many givers of punishment, is to deliver all kinds of punishment to the evil miscreants that are deserving of his wrath. The question is does He know the specifics of His responsibilities? And more importantly, who has given Him His duties? Further, if one has been judged as so evil that one should be kept out of and denied further physical existence then it is obviously just as important that YamaRaja understands and accepts all the workings of the spiritual world in order that He may help to keep the evil ones from returning to the physical world. Obviously this world is meant for those deserving of it.

The worst of it is I have a sneaking suspicion that this one called YamaRaja was never exactly charged directly with the mission of Death Lord. I think he may have become the President of the Council of Eternals without knowing of the similarities between it and the Lord of death. The Council of Eternals is a group of 700 men, all of them standing not much more than four feet tall! And yah, you might have guessed, they all wear little green jumpsuits with a symbol or badge over their heart that is exactly just as I will describe it. I believe that it is a circle with a star of David in it, and within that is an inverted swastika, which, curiously enough, did not actually originate with the Mighty (evil) Furor of Germany, as some of you may think, but was in existence long before that, in the Tibetan Book of the Dead some 4,000 years ago. The meaning of the symbols all combined, according to Elohim, is "that which is above is like that which is below, and everything is cyclic." The Council of Eternals is genuinely and precisely concerned with the well being of any and all who allow and may accept the supreme absolute truth through recognizing them as chanellers of that same truth all hearts have access to, thanks to the supreme pure energy (maya) of the original creator of creators, and equally mysterious Holy Ghost, Paramatma. Without maya, illusion and physical reality would not be possible, as that energy exists and permeates all physical reality.

Even though I think there may have been certain unfortunate conditions which either prevented them from receiving directly from their forefathers their personal karma, or perhaps they refused to listen to direction, somehow they seem to have instinctually picked up on what it is that they should be responsible for, as they did inherit a vast and amazing amount of technical knowledge and machinery that has given them the ability to perform various seemingly "magic" feats. Just before I go into great detail about all that, I think that it is important that I mention that the title we as Humans have given this YamaRaja character here on earth is "God", which is not only a name we have created for him, as opposed to a name he has chosen for himself, but according to him, is also a title which he himself is a little uncomfortable with, and we may find the word "God" more appropriately suits the entire collection of creators, yes that's right, creators. Indeed, contrary to popular and widespread belief, there was never ever just one creator of this and other planets and all that exists on, above, and within! Of this, you can be quite sure (I'd bet my life on it).

And so, that brings us basically back to the screen, which is presently still portraying the blackness of space, but for the brightness of the various luminous objects that decorate the otherwise empty space. Although there is much to say about the time and space before the beginning of the Council of Eternals, I want to be as brief as possible about it, as a lot has been either hidden or forgotten, and right now that is not the most important issue at hand. On that note, let's try to focus on the mysterious birth of perhaps one of the most famously controversial characters that has ever existed, and I intend to give you, the curious and true seeker, a clear picture of what it is like in the average and not so ordinary days in the life of the creator of that other famous fellow, Jesus Christ, and their associates, and just what life is like for them on their home world, somewhere approximately one light-year from Earth. Incidentally, Jehovah, the creator of Jesus, is also known as the God of Orion.

I would just like to include a little story of creation I heard told by a wise old sage I once encountered while on a journey hiking on the Himalayan mountains during the Fall. This is the story of the great Brahma[6] as it is transforming itself from one form, that of a spiritual nature, into another form, that of a physical nature. Right before Lord Brahma actually became a living physical entity, as was the natural habit of the Lord, being an accomplished daydreamer; the great hallucinator exercised his willpower and dreamed up this wonderful creation of his we now call "life." And quite a dream it was, because as he dreamed, his thought of dream state vision became manifest all throughout the universe around him...I mean like in, or seemingly on the apparent "backdrop" of darkness, the big screen of the universe. So gradually the Lord "drew" and projected his vision of creation, keeping a close eye on every little detail, making sure there were no mistakes or imperfections in the design. During the vision that the Yogi was having in a meditational state, which is the basis and origination of his story, the old Yogi received a vision of the outline of a man and a woman, drawn with stardust, somehow encased in another stardust "drawing" of the design of an hourglass. As the life of the "Great Spirit" and "Holy Ghost" seemed to enter into the both of them, they became alive with maya and as they grew alive, they started to reach for each other, as if to reach out and touch each other's fingers and hands. However, as they were trapped inside the image of the stardust hourglass, one on either side, it became impossible for each of the now physical shapes of the human beings to touch at all. There was no way for them to come together because the small hole that was between them was far too tiny for even a finger to reach through. This of course left the two feeling quite dismayed.

That's really as far as he went to explain his vision, he made no further effort to decipher the vision at all, leaving me to my imagination for any more detailed information regarding the true and complete meaning. The idea was that our creator basically used the universe itself as a sort of blackboard for its thoughts and ideas...first designing shapes and outlines in 'stardust' like one would first work with a blueprint, then letting this energy or maya bring the beings to life. This

---

[6] Sanskrit; the first created being of the universe; directed by Lord Vishnu, Brahma creates all life forms in the universe and rules the mode of passion.

method of creating would be a favorite amongst optimists and free thinkers. However, the Elohim have a more scientific approach to the matter, as you will see. It is easy for one to say that The Great Almighty Omnipotent original creative (God) force of the universe, etc., simply mustered up its willpower and imagined that certain ideas could exist, and therefore would exist, and so they did come to be simply because of the giant capability of that creative force to realize itself. I guess we would call it magic, to say the least, these days to be able to manifest a thought simply by willing it so. In fact, it's so easy to say, that it makes it that much harder to believe in. Who would have ever thought it could have been so easy? There is a lot to be said about the beginning of time, and some has been previously written about the beginning of existence, but it all really seems a lot less mysterious to me than a certain time period that came after the beginning.

This mysterious time began about the time of the birth of one YamaRaja, if indeed he was actually literally born into his world as the result of the actions of his biological parents, or if he came into being as a result of some kind of magical manipulation of creation by the DNA machine, it is not clear. Well, who or whatever was the predecessor of YamaRaja left him and his brothers a few very magical gifts, thereby endowing them with a great deal of power. This much is quite certain, and we can know this because of the testimony of Y.R. Himself. You see it is around this time that the most detailed information has most recently become available. And so again I leave you with the comfort of knowing that there are other writings about the very beginnings of existence. As he is growing, YamaRaja is told, as is everyone there, that they, on that planet, were left certain mechanical wonders, or rather, inherited these amazing machines that not only gives them the "power of eternity," let's say, but also gives them the ability to actually create from scratch, biologically, anything they can think of and apply their knowledge of DNA through the use of the machine they inherited. By the "power of eternity" I mean to say that they can live as long as they desire, even forever, if they really choose...simply by taking a DNA sample from a "retired" physical form and cloning, from that sample, another identical physical form. That same being can keep repeating the procedure every time its body grows old and dies, which only happens once every thousand years to the people of that planet. This is because of an injection that is given to them at the age of eighteen.

That's right; this magical elixir is a "fountain of youth" for them. One could say they are drinking from the fountain of eternal life. One could also wonder if Yama-Raja's predecessor's actually managed to impress upon him and some of his buddies, the huge amount of responsibility indicated by accepting the knowledge and power one actually does by adopting the continual usage of such wonderful machines. By doing so, one is actually opting out of the natural process of death and rebirth, if you happen to believe in that sort of thing, which according to his very own statement recently made in 1976, I believe, the very one that I think, unknown to himself it seems, is supposed to be YamaRaja, doesn't believe. In his book, Rael quoted him, as saying that there is no life after death as so many of us believe. He said that contrary to what we believe, once you die, that's it...there is nothing else you cease to exist. In other words they have, in the past anyway been living in denial of the soul, not really believing in it or reincarnation.

Needless to say, this came as a bit of a shock to me, personally. I've always believed that the physical form is a great gift; nevertheless, it seems to expire after a certain amount of continual usage. But for those who so simply seem to choose to believe, there is far more to do with the gift of Atma than to mindlessly give it up and away to anyone to do with as they please, regardless of Atma. Anyway, that was some years ago, and so, it's still possible He may have changed His beliefs since then; if not, he may be convinced otherwise some time in the future. There will remain hope until then, I'm sure. In the meantime, we must accept the fact that YamaRaja and His friends on that nameless planet one light-year from Earth, according to Yama-Raja Himself, believe that the only way to live beyond one lifespan, be it either one of a thousand years, as it is on their planet, or one of not much more than one hundred years, as it is here on Earth, he says, the only way for one to "live" beyond that time is if the Council of Eternals decides that they should, and consequently grants them eternal life via their magical mechanical methods, or machines that they inherited. Again, should they decide that you deserve it, they would simply clone you from a cellular DNA sample, retrieved preferably from a one inch square piece of bone from your forehead, or a piece of skin or something that contains an accurate imprint of your personal DNA code (they prefer the small piece of bone). In fact, if need be, they even have the technology to recreate you from a photograph of you! Imagine that! Simply by feeding the information the photograph provides into the machine and pressing a button, out comes an exact replica of the person in the photograph! Of course, the magical workings of the machine are not confined to the limitations of using photographs to feed it the information. One can also program the machine using nothing but the limitations of your personal individual creativity and imagination. Yes, you simply decide first of all which gender you're looking to create, and then what color its skin will be, and hair color, eyes, etc., and the relative measurements of the being, and so on and so forth until you've completely designed the individual being quite to your liking and exacting specifications.

This reminds me again of that wise old sage I was telling you about before, and during that same vision, the yogi was seeing the creation of the universe; you know, solar giants, black holes, intense balls of immensely huge fire, all blending and mixing together in the vast darkness of seemingly endless outer space. And after this tremendous and furious scurrying about of energy, it all seemed aesthetically symmetrical, containing within its balanced self the outline of a body, somehow having for its eyes the sun and moon.

Assuming this to be the body of Krishna, with a sun and moon as the eyes of its head, and the rest of its body being made up of the remaining entire created universe, we can also imagine the heart of this giant universal body to be the most likely position for Goloka Vrndavana[7]. As it is with the human body, the Paramatma resides in the heart, watching over its host and material creation. It is good to know that there is somewhere to go to even though it may well be in another dimension, if one should so desire, that is to say, if one tires of the physical universe, there is always that spiritual retreat.

And so, summoning the creative powers from within themselves, the inheritors of the DNA machine may have designed their first beings, fashioned after their own DNA patterns, with only a few changes or experimental modifications. One of those experimental adjustments was to the relative size of the being, in relation to themselves who

---

[7] Sanskrit; the eternal transcendental (spiritual) abode of (the Holy Spirit), Lord Krishna

happened to be designed, quite conveniently I think, to reach the basic maximum height of four feet. Anyway, they took it upon themselves to imagine races of humans of varying height. One of these races is reported as being around fourteen feet tall. Personally, I have got to sympathize with the giants...I can't imagine what it must be like for those of them who might be experiencing a little, or a lot of back pain (like me). So for this reason alone, I envy those little guys just a bit. However, I also have come to the conclusion that they most likely began experimenting with the genetic manipulation through the use of the machine by examining the results of some very imaginative, and I might say, highly successful little creators. However, as you may have noticed, they have also learned how to be equally efficient masters of destruction. In fact, it is partially due to the more destructive sides of a few of the members of the Council of Eternals that a very large part of this planet we all know and love, Earth, has been inhabited and populated, thanks to a whole lot of effort on their part. Just before I explain what exactly I mean in the previous statement, I'd like to take the time to define the difference in meaning between the words Alien and Extraterrestrial according to my cosmic glossary of intergalactic words given to me by my personal and trusted, not to mention highly respected and loved cosmic contact (who shall remain nameless at this point in the story, although I may give him a nickname later if he keeps popping up). So, let's ask ourselves, what is an E.T.? And the answer should be "any entity that knows how to love," as compared to an Alien, who is any being that does not yet know, or understand love and the necessity of love, and further, this usually would refer to any being that would originate somewhere other than our planet Earth. So from here on in, I will be referring to those no longer wondering what the difference is, as the friendly E.T.s and the rather unfriendly ones as Aliens. That brings us back to the story of our friendly little fellow who has become the President of the Council of Eternals, or at least, an account of his story according to him as of the year 1976.

Chapter 2

The Killing Arena

Whether or not his account of things is 100% accurate or not is debatable. However I'm going to tell you his version, as well as another possible version. According to Yama-Raja, he was told as a youngster (keeping in mind that he lives to be 1,000 years on his planet), that they had been the happy recipients of a time capsule that they had discovered drifting through space, and recovering the floating, perhaps lost time capsule the Elohim found the capsule to contain the information necessary for eternal survival and creation. And so, this strange planet one light year from Earth is populated by some 7 billion people, of which I believe, only 700 of them being of the four foot tall species, having a fairly dark olivecoloured complexion, and wholly comprising the makeup of the Council of Eternals. The remaining percentage ratio of average humans to B.R.s (Biological Robots) is unknown to me exactly, but it is safe to say that at least 50% of them are just as normal in appearance to the earth human, as another being from Earth. Some of them are fairskinned, others are not so fair, but darker in complexion. But it seems they all speak the same language on their still unnamed planet, and I've yet to hear a common or singular name for the language they speak either, but Yama-Raja tells us again in '76 of its similarity to the language of the Greeks and Israelites here on Earth.

And so the Elohim went about their business populating their planet and experimenting with their genetic creations until they where either tired, or simply had enough on their planet to deal with. Some of the Council's members saw fit to create a certain type of animal, such as a unicorn or giraffe or something, others were content with creating some kind of plant, vegetable, tree, or flower. On that planet, some of the creators were able to design flowers that could change colours and give off amazingly beautiful and pungent aromas. As you walk, or fly around the planet, you can smell many different and pleasing scents as well as hearing lots of different kinds of music coming from seemingly nowhere. You'll also come across the aforementioned B.R.s.

These Biological Robots are normal in every other appearance to the human, except for the blue rock that is embedded into the forehead of the individual B.R. right between the eyes of the being, thereby permitting the entity to be controlled by its designer/creator/master. Not everyone has a B.R. as a slave for normal slave duties, or as sexual servants, designed specifically by the Master according to his/her specifications. Some humans are content with their other human counterparts. Of course, there, one is allowed to do just as one pleases, within reason of course. In fact, those who cannot control their own tempers are dealt with severely, as the Council doesn't tolerate unnecessary violence. People, or individuals who cannot control their anger and aggression toward others are put into a huge circular enclosure style stage with lots of seats for the audience to watch as the overly aggressive individuals are made to fight to the death in competition style performances. I think it's also safe to say that these folks are serious about peace. I also mentioned earlier that as you walked or "flew"…well, make no mistake, I literally meant to say that it is possible for you to actually fly instead of walking or driving. Well, when I say fly, I mean without a huge encompassing clumsy entrapment of any kind of machine to worry about piloting. You simply strap on a special kind of belt around your waist, and away you go…carried up on some kind of energy beam, people travel to and fro going about their business, and doing what they do, to fill their many days of existence on that planet.

I should mention that they on that planet are also very advanced technically in the field of medicine. Sometimes for that reason, certain individuals that live there may take a greater risk than you might think they should, simply because the advanced medical doctors can repair easily any kind of damage and injury, or if a person dies, that same one can be easily cloned and made to live again for a thousand years!

As a result of this rather risqué lifestyle, the people of that planet have learned to devise some very dangerous sports and activities. Such activities include a popular and favored sport enjoyed by many a driving enthusiast...the Atomic sports car races. In this hair raising event, also watched by many spectators, if any of the people involved become injured in any way, they know that it is relatively simple to have the repairs done.

There is another advantage to the invention and usage of the antigravity belt, and that is the practical convenience it brings with it to normal everyday living conditions. Well, normal that is if you happen to live in their world. I say that because of their unusual and innovative style of living in multifamily complexes. Let me explain what I mean. They live in 2km square buildings that are hollowed out in the center in terms of having any kind of floor, except for around the outside of the building on the very edge of it where there is just enough room for the number of people living there to bed down after a long day, or simply whenever it is necessary for them to snooze a little and regenerate their bodily functions that rely on sleep for recuperation. If I remember correctly, He also states in His story as told to Rael, that they have no night and day phenomena as we here on Earth do, but that instead, there, sunlight can be controlled from their planet, in terms of varying degrees, and just how long they desire sunlight. Therefore it seems they have chosen to keep the thing shining all the time. It is also not uncommon to encounter a couple along the way casually engaged in one of the numerous stages of ecstasy and arousal experienced during sex. Oh yes, I think it's probably only fair to warn you that on that planet, as we do here, you will most likely come upon bisexual, homosexual, and heterosexual people in your journey.

Well, by now you're all getting a pretty clear picture of what life must be like for the average individual on that loka[8], however, there are still a few things that I would like to tell you before we go on. I

---

[8]   Sanskrit; planet.

feel it is just as important to be prepared for the possible future, as it is to know about where we might have come from. This, I dare say, is not the first time you've taken interest in outer space my friend, and certainly shouldn't be the last. Remember the popular show Star Trek? Well, they say that that program also is working with hidden but not unobvious messages. Things like the Holodeck, tractor beams, and antigravity beams are very real and in use already by the E.T.s. Indeed these hidden messages are meant to prepare us for the future. For instance, the E.T.s indeed have the ever-popular shields around their ships to protect them from alien laser blasts. In fact I've got a very interesting, action packed story to relate to y'all later in this story that pertains directly to the advantages of equipping our pilots with these shields or force fields around their crafts. One of the unique features of the Pleiadian crafts is the way in which they do their laundry on board a mother ship. One simply steps into a little room with their clothes on and a special light comes on and bathes you and your garb for a few seconds. Viola! No more dirty, smelly laundry.

As you might well guess, there is a lot of laying around, literally, as well as just getting laid, although it is no longer necessary for the fornicator to be relying upon their bed space to "make out" with their lover. With great thanks to the inventor of the antigravity belts, it is possible for the lovers to "fly united," or do it in midair! Sounds like the kind of place I might like to visit, I'm sure, especially knowing that my true first love of passing time, which is an important decision to realize, is the creating of music, and of course the performance of it, etc. I think a person like me could actually learn to enjoy a thousand years of life, living it in such a manner.

The best part, in all practicality, is undoubtedly the fact that all the food that one could possibly consume or desire is free. That is to say it comes to you at no actual financial cost absolutely free. Now tell me you couldn't get used to that! I guess that if one is religiously spiritual, you may question the necessity of the B.R.s as slaves. You may also wonder what, if any, suffering may be incurred upon that soul enslaved. However, I'm quite sure the people of that planet really believe the B.R.s have no soul. Just as they seem to think that all of us are spiritless as they've previously allowed their leader to state. Of course, it's not mandatory to possess a slave there, and neither is it mandatory to do anything really, except to be relatively peaceful, of course. And they encourage individuals to nurture some kind of creative, possibly productive atmosphere, as the Council members themselves are often busy with some kind of creation or invention. Even now they are working to improve their ability to travel through space. More precisely, they are presently capable of traveling through space at the approximate maximum speed of 8 times the speed of light. Before long however, maybe even now, they'll be traveling at a top approximate speed of 11 times the speed of light!

If you're wondering what kind of food these people eat, it's very much the same as what you're already used to. Basically the average diet of the Elohim consists of a lot of small animals like rabbits and fowl for protein and meat. Naturally they eat lots of veggies and fruits and grains, etc. I suppose those who enjoy preparing their own food do just so, and others would probably use a B.R. slave to do it. There is one other requirement for the loving couple that live together, whether in marriage or not, and that is that they, as a couple, procreate and actually conceive only two children per family. This is obviously due to the amount of people already living there and the relative amount of space that is left. I must say it's probably a good idea, although I would personally love "to go where no one has gone before," in search of new places to live, and civilizations to uncover, and charter maps of the universe. I don't know exactly how important it is for them to go on scouting missions like that, if at all, as I'm sure more than one race of E.T.s has the ability to create entire new planets and also have control over micro and macroclimate.

In fact, there was a time when certain citizens of their planet were forced in exile to flee to another place in the universe to survive and live. Again, a most important time and event in history, as this is the reason a lot of us are here today, believe it or not! Yes, it seems that our hero Yama-Raja, or Jehovah, some call him, which means the same thing as Yahweh, I'm sure (one with no name), yes it seems our little hero didn't spend all of his youth time days lounging around on animal furs in the sun, watching the naked beauties dancing to the invisible music for his pleasure, showing off their bodies as he nibbled on pieces of toasted meats and tasty fruits. No, methinks he's spent a little time himself encouraging his own creativity and inventiveness. This is quite obvious as we take into consideration the account of his autobiography, as told to Rael, again back in 1976.

All in all, it really seems to be an all right place. Basically, one might even venture to say, in agreement with all of them, that their planet is far more advanced technically, and although I find it hard to take, that for the most part, I'd have to say that their society as a whole is also evolved slightly further than ours appears to be, in terms of world peace anyway…and brotherly acceptance and all, you know, that sort of thing. My imagination paints a very pretty picture when I think of all the painters, sculptors, artists of any kind including musicians, and anything else you can think of like gardeners and tailors, although there is a lot of nakedness there, and oh yes, let's not forget our scientists and philosophers and even doctors. With the amount of encouragement and support they seem to be getting from the Council, it paints a pretty picture indeed. Nevertheless, that's only in my imagination at this point, as I can't help remembering the way history is really written. Indeed it has taken a different path from all that dreamy utopian projection, just how different, I'm about to explain.

It's my guess that during the course of creative endeavors with their discovered DNA machine, that there may have been a certain amount of competition amongst the 700 members of the Council, especially in the areas of overall strength and even meanness of certain more aggressive animals they created. Even in the smaller animals they designed they were careful to devise at least some sort of protection from the larger and nastier animals. It's just as likely that there was a certain amount of competition of a different sort, like who could design the prettiest flower or bird, or perhaps even inventing the flower, herb, or spice that produced the nicest and most pleasing aroma. Then there must have also been a different level of competition again; only in the area of, let's says…practicality, of some plant or healing herb that could have a specific duty or precise purpose in terms of preventative medicine or any other kind of treatment. Although I'm not really sure who came up with the idea for the elixir of eternal life. That was a good one. My most sincere congratulations and personal thanks go out to the inventor of it. Whether or not it came on the time capsule, or it was discovered after that by the Elohim, or even one of the other neighboring intergalactic space beings and passed on to them some time, for some reason. Methinks again, that it's most likely to have come to them along with other knowledge, if you can believe the time capsule story at all. There are other possibilities you know. I'm not saying that our little friends from far away are lying to us, but I'm merely suggesting that their peers, or most recent ancestors to the direct inheritors of the information of the time capsule, may have told them a little white lie in order to protect their own feelings as well as those of their offspring.

It's quite possible that YamaRaja's superiors were not his real biological parents who inherited for their family the time capsule at all, but instead created the time capsule themselves and sent it up before they actually produced the members of the Council of Eternals, to orbit their planet and be 'discovered' by them at a later date. I mean suppose his 'parents' did actually create them all from scratch using the DNA machine for a very specific purpose, and feared that their newly created beings might revolt and reject, perhaps even resent the fact that they had been created and destined for an eternity of duties and responsibilities. In essence feeling that they themselves were no different than a biological robot except that they didn't have the little blue "persuasion" embedded in their foreheads to convince them, and to make sure they were willing to cooperate with their superiors. So they cleverly devised an elaborate ruse to deceive their little helpers, in hopes that they would not harbor any resentment towards their creators and therefore, perhaps, be more willing to participate in various activities if they believed it was all some luck, some unforeseen fortune bestowed upon them all quite by chance.

Actually, the more I think about it the more I realize that there may be more than one other possible explanation that could explain everything. Again, I suppose I should do what I usually do when hearing a story for the first time and wondering whether or not there is more than one version of the story (and of course, which explanation is the correct one and perhaps even why one should doubt the story teller in the first place), and that is to just believe. My friends often caution me on this very matter and suggest I might try to be a little more cautious, and perhaps a little less gullible. Yeah...I actually thought of at least two other versions of his original story before I stopped to question why I had even ever doubted the first version as told to Rael by

Jehovah in 1976, as they chatted atop a French mountain range, sitting comfortably together in his two seater aircraft, or I.F.O. (Identified Flying Object), which by the way was of the kind of craft that could travel 8x the speed at which light travels (but soon to be improved to 11x light speed).

The aircraft also had another neat little feature: the type of windows in use. They sport a very interesting and impressive feature or method of operation. That is to say that when you desire to have a little look-see, out and about, all you have to do is put your hand near the window, or touch it gently and whoosh! The place you're touching that was once a wall, suddenly and surprisingly transforms into a completely transparent metallic window! It is really just as I said: a window that is actually a type of metal that can be made transparent. Now if that isn't just the niftiest invention since sliced bread and catnip...what is? Well, I'll give you a suggestion that might be a close runner to the 'magic' windows, and that is how they fly their spacecraft. I'll tell you, there is a lot more to their crafts than you might think. Just to get one of these things through the initial ignition procedures is one thing in itself. Then one has to deal with the feat of actually piloting the craft. And although basic and relatively simplistic, and very practical ideals are efficiently doing the job, there are a few extremely important details the pilot must learn, as there is not going to be anyone else there to help you, the pilot, if you should fail to remember some specific function or detail. Some ships however, do require a complicated series of clearance procedures as well, and even programming details from a home base station, including details for the actual flight pattern, and speed factors, which affect the e.t.a. In fact, I can show you an exact set of flight instructions for a particular craft, that I believe is hidden somewhere on this Earth, but let's worry about that later.

As well, there are in fact "scout ships" that are indeed sent out from "mother ships" for certain scouting missions. Some of them can be remotely controlled, and are therefore pilot-less. Others are oneseaters and are typically used in battles. These are the ones I was referring to when I said that there would be nobody there to help you make any kind of immediate decision or assist you with any action other than voice contact, so it's up to you to make all the right moves if you want to keep yourself airborne. It is thankfully, relatively simple to operate these machines, I believe, anyway, according to what I have been lucky enough to discover. I've actually observed quite a lot of interesting maps, documents, and other details of some very interesting and innovative designs, plans, and accounts of journeys and adventures that certain lucky individuals were fortunate enough to have been involved in. Some of the extraterrestrial activities and events are not so exciting, others far more hair raising than you could possibly imagine. You may have already heard some or all of the stories I'm about to relate to y'all. Then again, this could all be completely and entirely new to you, and therefore you have become as curious as I did, and began to listen to stories and research, and read any kind of relative material that is at hand, in order to supplement your knowledge of extraterrestrial activities and phenomenon. I should therefore continue with my account of basically all, or most of the knowledge I have discovered over the course of approximately 35 years of researching and studying literature and reports from various sources, most of all which I'd rather not reveal the identify of, for obvious reasons and concerns.

I mentioned briefly before secret messages that are hidden within the natural fibers of the modern day outer space programs on television, such as the ever-popular Star Trek, like the transporter beam, which in reality is blue in colour. Star Trek, and other outer space shows from T.V. and the big screen do indeed contain "plants", or clues within the story line that hint at events that are yet to come in our very real future and everyday life in order to prepare us for just such an occasion, or at least, those of us who believe they may want or deserve to experience some extraterrestrial activity.

Still another very real clue is the "tractor beam," or antigravity beam, which can be used for lifting heavy objects such as people, animals, rocks, perhaps a vehicle, or an iceberg you might imagine being transported right in the middle of a desert nearby in order to irrigate the landscape and save any native residents that might just happen to be living in the area. Or one could even speculate that such a device as the antigravity beam would have been used in the construction of the mysterious and spectacular pyramids that have just as mysteriously appeared on various locations scattered about our planet. And not only on our planet Earth, but on a neighboring planet as well: the surface of the planet in our system that we know to be called Mars (according to, and with great surprise, the recent photographs taken and returned to Earth "magically" by one of the American satellites, "Viking" I believe, that was up there orbiting our planet for one reason or another).

By now, everybody with a television here on Earth has probably seen the photographs, or perhaps those without television might have seen pictures in a magazine, or newspaper, or even all of the above. At any rate, what it is, is what appears to be a series of more that one pyramid on the surface of the planet Mars. On one of the structures there seems to be what looks just like a huge and very familiar looking face of an individual that has the very distinct resemblance of what was built here on Earth in the county that we call Egypt. And that familiar looking face is the resemblance of that huge head that is on the statue of the Sphinx.

I believe that at least one of the pyramids that were recently spotted by the satellite in the Sedonia region on Mars is a five-sided pyramid. There is no doubt, in my mind anyway, that all of these pyramids were built with assistance of the heavenly gods, if not entirely by the gods themselves. But what reasons(s) inspired the creators of these wondrous structures? Well there are many theories and ideas about the purposes of these structures, and I think that it is safe to say that there is more than one purpose for the pyramid.

There has also been a great deal of speculation as to just what exactly might be there at the site of the pyramid structures on Mars, especially the one with the 3D face that appears to be staring up from the surface of the planet as if it is actually observing something, or perhaps watching over something. Or is it someone? Or perhaps that big giant face that seems to actually change its expression as the light and shadows paint the face according to the relative position of the surrounding planets, sun, and stars...perhaps that face is watching over a whole bunch of people, and maybe even doing more than just watching.

In fact, we may choose to wonder no longer, and accept the explanation offered consisting of evidence that suggests that indeed the giant face is doing just that, and behaving as if it were some sort of guardian angel that oversees the activities on and surrounding our dear planet Earth. I believe that the information is true and that states that there is a space base that does exist under the surface of the planet Mars, and is inhabited at least temporarily, and is merely part of a larger group of E.T.s that are concerned about us, and have banded together with one common idea. That is to protect the people of this planet Earth as much as possible from these very real and evil alien forces that are also drawn towards us here on Earth, for very different reasons. They do not intend to do that all by themselves, far from it, comparatively they are a small portion of a much larger group of guardians encircling this planet, and placing themselves at strategic locations all around us. With their technology, they have devised ways to construct underground hideaways under the surface of other planets in our solar system as well, so that they are not visible. As I've already explained, we, the people of Earth, for the most part are completely unaware of how fortunate we really are and have been in the past. For they have saved all of our lives more than once, and I think we all owe them, at least, our gratitude, as they have risked their own lives over and over in order to save ours...and until now, we didn't even know it!

Well, that is most of us didn't know until now. How many of you really did? And how many of you really care? I'm talking to the skeptics among you, when I ask, if you understand how frustrating it can be, simply presenting a hypothetical situation to a real skeptical thinker? For instance; using the logic of the typical skeptic concerning the question of who built the pyramids, I mean, according to a skeptical person, they must have been constructed by the slaves of the Egyptians...therefore, by that same logic, they, the slaves, must also have built the pyramids that we have recently discovered on Mars' surface. But even you, the skeptic, must know that just isn't likely.

Looking along the angle of the shafts that extend from the actual room or tombs that contain the sarcophagus, we can see that the shafts lead, or point directly towards certain stars in the constellation Orion. Now if you look closely at that same constellation, you'll notice that it lies directly beside the Milky Way, and from that same image, we can see an exact reflection of that picture, or mirror image from the scene in the sky, directly below the heavens, back along the shaft angle, upon the ground in Egypt. Many of you probably already know that from above, in the air, it has been noticed that the pyramids themselves are laid out upon the ground in such a manner as to make a pattern, exactly the same as the pattern of the stars that make up the constellation of Orion, and upon looking a little further, we can see that the Nile

River seems to look exactly like the Milky Way looks next to Orion. Now we can see that the pattern that is formed upon the ground, or the mirror image of the heavens, is only visible from high above the Earth itself, in the air. Besides all of this, that obviously suggests that somebody was flying around during those days, it just seems to me that the weight of those stones would have been too great for the slaves to move alone. Well, I don't know why I'm even trying to sway anybody's decision here anyway...once somebody makes up their mind to ignore certain obvious evidence, there is usually a reason that they don't want to believe anyway.

I do believe that it is really quite unlikely those primitive people are entirely responsible for the construction of the pyramids. Further, I suggest to you that they could not have accomplished such a great feat without the assistance and direction of a technologically advanced society and their superior equipment. All of this evidence does suggest that the race of people most likely responsible for the project were quite capable of not only flying, but also moving extremely heavy objects with relative ease…most likely by using a device such as an antigravity beam. Thinking back to the angle shafts that lead from the King's and Queen's chambers, up and out through the walls of the pyramids, aiming directly towards the stars, this evidence would seem to indicate this same race of advanced beings were also a very spiritual people, as they seemed to be greatly concerned with the return of the souls of the rulers to Orion. I have to say, there seems to be a little more to the pyramids than just the amazing preserving qualities for dead bodies, and anything else one puts in it. Yes indeed, it would seem that they are actually watching over us and have helped us thwart off many would-be attackers of the plant Earth in the past, along with the help of some others that are concerned for our wellbeing. This whole entire group of "guardian angels," lets call them, is comprised of enough of them to form an actual circle around us here on our planet Earth. Thus, they form a protective ring around us, protecting us from anything that might not have our best interests at heart. Because of their careful positioning around us, they are able to see and intercept, if necessary, anything or anyone that enters our atmosphere or poses a threat to us in any way at all. There is absolutely no way whatsoever that any kind of evil force can invade our galaxy undetected, and it is not because they haven't tried that we haven't seen them, believe me. In fact, right beside the famous star we call the North Star, which is very visible in the night sky; there exists a space base that was created around the time of the civilization of the great Atlantis. The name of the space base is Alpha Centauri believe it or not. Anyway, Alpha Centauri, the base, is still used today by the E.T.s as a stopover point for anyone traveling to Earth, and of course, it is also used by the guardian angels who are caring enough for some of us here on Earth to spend all of their time away from their home world and risk their lives just to oversee those of us here that may deserve a chance to believe in them, in civilization, I suppose, and in the name of Jiva.

CHAPTER 3

Jehovah's Exile

We have learned from the past that during difficult times here on Earth we should not be surprised to find that there may be some kind of helpful intervention from the E.T.s, especially if there is a great catastrophe ahead for us that could spell out the end of civilization, as it was for the people of Atlantis many years ago when their continent sank beneath the sea. At that time, there was a league of E.T.s that decided they would risk their lives as well, in hopes that they might be able to convince at least some of the people of Atlantis that they still had a chance to survive if they could trust their space "brothers" and sisters" enough to allow them to help them. Although I'm sure it didn't take too much convincing for some of them, even though they knew of the impending doom, there were still some who, for whatever reason, stayed behind and died when the land sank under the water. But with the help of the E.T.s and their newly designed space base near the North Star, the believers were able to continue living. This can explain where at least some of our ancestors have come from, as they were lifted by the E.T.s through the air, via spacecraft, all the way to North and South America, where they could be safe for some time and have another chance at continuing their species. This might also explain some of the similarities noticed between the ancient Mayan civilization and the Atlantians, and why the Mayan people seemed to worship certain gods that came from the sky. With all this protection we as Earth people seem to have, you might well ask or wonder, just how is it then that there has been so much already said about certain groups of aliens that would indeed appear to be evil? Well, if you recall carefully, you will remember that I did mention a protective ring around our planet. However that protected and closely monitored area is only to include that space around us we call our Galaxy. As yet, the E.T.s have not begun to offer us here on the surface of the planet any kind of real protection in general from the evil forces that may be dwelling here amongst us. For the most part, they are still leaving it up to us to take care of such things.

As most of you probably already have heard, there was, or should I say is, this little fellow that we know as Satan, who was once living among those that come from the sky that we now know to be the Elohim. In the Bible it says that this fellow, Lucifer, was once an angel living in Heaven with God and the rest of the angels. This is how it was until he, (the Devil), sinned against them and was kicked out of Heaven and sent down to Earth to live amongst us here and, as if that wasn't enough, God had to go and give him the power to rule over the monetary system! And so, this is how it is still, to this day. Satan remains one of the, if not the most threatening of the dangers, or seemingly evil forces living amongst us here on good old Terra Firma.

I really don't know what He was thinking when He did that. Well, I suppose He wanted to give him something to occupy himself so he wouldn't be tempted to come back and hassle everyone, or anybody, on their home world. Satan obviously hadn't sinned to the extent that he deserved to be put to death and have a sample of his DNA stored away for possible future use. I mean in case they decided they wanted to clone him and bring him back to life for punishment or for whatever reason. At any rate, YamaRaja and his associates decided to exile Satan who was actually one of the 700 members that make up the Council of Eternals. I don't know if they ever found it necessary to find a replacement for the exiled one or not, but if they should ever decide to do so, if they haven't already, I think there can only be...

two possible candidates, and those that most likely would be chosen would be either Jesus, the devoted messenger of his creator, Jehovah, or the Great Granddaddy of them all, and original creator of the entire universe, the one that existed even before, (and) created time...the one the Bible itself calls the "Holy Ghost."

Amazingly enough, it would seem that Satan was not the only fellow to be exiled from the Council, yeah, believe it or not, his famous counterpart, and some of his closest buddies on the Council also managed to get themselves thrown out of Heaven. This I think y'all will find most interesting and really obviously quite relevant to our present day civilization and the entire history of the planet earth. Without a doubt, this account of things, as they were, will explain a lot in really a very few words. As it is the truth as spoken by the creator of Jesus, I think it can be considered important and probably true.

Without further ado, I'll begin to tell you that these few close friends of YamaRaja and Yama-Raja Himself were not content with creating the kinds of things that all of the other members were creating. I also wonder about the practical sensibilities of some of the creators that were coming up with things like lions and tigers and great poisonous snakes, etc., or even what possible intention they had in their minds if in fact they did come up with deadly poisonous killer plants and herbs. I suppose it all could have come from the competitive nature of the whole affair, you know, just as they were also involved in very competitive sports and other competitions, like who could develop the prettiest flower or the nicest smelling herb or tastiest spice or foodstuff...certain members amongst them took it upon themselves to design the nastiest and most ferocious beast that could devour or otherwise destroy the "other guy's" creature. I think that may probably be closer to how their creative ideas evolved on that world. And that is how, I think, these fellows came up with the infamous dinosaur, and other prehistoric creatures. It's not that I think they created the dinosaurs; it's just that I think their competitive nature drove them to such lengths; it is fact that they did actually create the dinosaurs, according to YamaRaja, although, they may not have been the very first creators of these ancient and scary creatures. He Himself says that is the primary reason for the exile of Him and His friends. They were asked by their peers to either stop manipulating the DNA so as to create these huge and horrific creatures, or they would have to face being exiled from the planet and home world. Quite obviously they chose to continue with their experiments, even if it meant that they would be kicked out of Heaven. And that's exactly what did happen to Yama-Raja and his friends, because they had refused to discontinue their dinosaur experimenting, they were forced off of their home planet by their superiors, who had also been those same people responsible for telling Yama-Raja and the others that they had all inherited the time capsule from some unknown source. All this, of course, makes me wonder how YamaRaja, eventually became the President of the Council of Eternals. Obviously His exile was not a permanent one, because he did in fact return to become the beloved president. I wonder where his superiors were then, when he returned, and why they themselves didn't retain that title. If everyone there lives forever, you would think that any peers would remain in a position of leadership once there. I wonder where their superiors are now and what happened to them right after the exiled ones returned?

I mentioned before that certain individuals had managed to get themselves exiled from Heaven, well, perhaps I should elaborate a bit more in regard to the few certain details that I have managed to acquire relative to two or three particularly famous ones amongst the exiled, and perhaps I should mention as well that the exact time of exile differed slightly. I mean that the lot of them were all exiled at the same time for their continuing to experiment with the dinosaur DNA but even after their return the first time, which, incidentally could never have happened without the help of the civilization of the people of Earth, there was a second exile, and that was to the one we call "Satan." At this time the devil did take up residence 200 km.s under the surface of the earth, more precisely, directly beneath the South Pole! Incredibly, he's built a huge underground complex there and flies in and out at will, almost, with the use of his particular type of spacecraft. I'll tell you more about that later.

First I want to get into a little more detail about the first period of exile. As I said, a small group of them were sent on their way to find a suitable planet for them to continue with their DNA experiments. It just so happened, that the planet that they decided to occupy for the next little while was our planet, Earth. Now at that time, so they say, our planet was covered by a lot of water; in fact, the entire surface of the earth was under water. Anyway, there was enough water covering the surface to prompt them to set off a series of very huge and powerful explosions that would create huge landmasses and mountains out of the ocean depths. Miraculously they managed to cause these large masses of land to rise to, and out of, the surface of the water with their obviously very powerful bombs. It seems that their elders didn't send them away empty handed or unprepared. That is how the story in the Bible came to be in Genesis, in the beginning where it says God did cause the firmament to rise from the depths between the waters and the waters. As the story goes He, and His friends in exile did then go about populating their newly created garden with the first of their created humans to walk the earth and call it home, and indeed they created Eve from a DNA sample out of Adam's rib.

While we're on a roll here, I might just attempt to clear up a few other simple mysterious but well-known occurrences from the story of the Bible. I suppose it only makes a little more sense if I try to keep these few events in chronological order. So I've basically explained the underlying reason that they came upon the planet Earth already, as they were all in a state of exile, they happened to come upon it and decided it would be suitable to fulfill their needs and purposes. I suppose it will also be relevant to the situation to know as well, that at the time of the parting of the sea for Moses and his merry band of followers, that whole amazing and certainly spectacular event, or "illusion," some might call it, was actually created from up above them in the clouds, where, hiding behind the cover of the clouds, "God" and his buddies were able to part the actual Red sea with the use of some kind of an antigravity beam that was projected from their spacecraft, contrary to popular belief that God did it all by Himself without the help of the use of the spaceship and its "magical" wondrous devices. Not that the Great and Holy Spirit couldn't do it just by willing it to happen, I suppose, I mean if it really wanted to. Anyway, that wasn't the only time they did conceal their craft from view behind the cover of the clouds. From that position they were also able to help their faithful friend and messenger, Jesus, to perform what would seem to be "miracles." In fact they helped him to perform these miracles on many different occasions, and were able to themselves stay hidden away from the general masses of people that were actually following their friend Jesus. Like the time He was able to produce thousands of fish for all his hungry followers and change their water into wine, of course again without the knowledge of their secret ways, one would hardly suspect them, or him, of any sort of trickery, but after you learn the real truth behind the situation, and possibly even forgive their deceptions and even come to an understanding of the deeper scope or perspective of the plot.

At the risk of shortening the entire length of this project, I'm going to "dive right in," so to speak and tell you the few other things that I can as quickly, and as clearly as possible, without messing it up with my personal perspective or feelings about the matter. I do want to leave you with a clear and easy to understand picture of the whole situation, and of course, I would like to keep it all as objective as I possibly can so that you may reach your own conclusions and opinions about it all at the end. I think one of the best "tricks" that Jesus and his creator played on their followers, next to the disappearing act of course, was the time when he hopped out of the boat that a half dozen or so of his closest followers were riding in, and proceeded with great ease, to walk out onto the surface of the water, without sinking down under. Of course such an act would astonish anyone without the correct and true details of how he actually did it. And so they indeed were astonished by the performance and undoubtedly, the trick made believers out of all or most of them. If only they had been told by him previous to doing it that there was indeed a type of flying craft hiding up in the clouds, and was projecting a beam out from under it that was an anti-gravity beam, invisible to their naked eyes of course, that was holding him up and keeping him from sinking below the surface, or swimming back to the boat, yes well, things would certainly have taken a different course in history.

I really don't understand the great lengths they went to, in order to convince us all to become "believers" or Christians, especially considering the nasty death that Jesus had to suffer, and all for us, how selfless. Of course there are those who believe that He did not actually die on the cross. Apparently, He was taken down from it early and allowed to fake his death so that he could go on living with the love of his life, Mary Magdalene. Together they may have migrated to

France and raised a large family that claims a direct lineage to them even to this day. For obvious reasons this would have been kept very much a secret and still is. If you would like to read about this further and hear a very good argument for that theory, I highly recommend reading one of Sylvia Browne's books called "Secrets and Mysteries of the World". I don't think it was all really necessary, especially in view of the facts around and concerning the Tower of Babylon. That in itself is an occasion which offers proof that not only did the people of Earth believe in God, but they in fact obviously cared about Him as well. They even cared enough about Him to help Him petition His own superiors that remained, still on their home planet and world, one light year from the planet where Jehovah and his closes buddies were exiled. In fact, at that time, the people of Earth did petition the people who had actually exiled Jehovah and company, so that they might be able to return to their once "home" and be there again with those that they had missed, but once lived with and, I suspect, loved. If it had not been for the sincere efforts of those dedicated Earthlings, and or perhaps I should call them Christians, to convince his peerage that they had indeed learned their lesson and were treating them, their creation, properly and with respect, they may not have been able to return to their beloved home world. But it seems the testimony of the faithful earthlings moved the people responsible for the exile, into changing their minds and allowing the exiled ones to return to their home planet once again, and have since then, somehow become more than important and indeed...they are considered VIPs. Even with and considering all of the aforementioned secrets now exposed, so that we may see them in the true light, as they really happened, it may sometimes be still difficult to understand each and every little action on the part of our ancestors and creators. There may still come to us a mystery as to why God behaves the way that He does, or seems to, but, if all of this can be accepted as the truth, until such a time as an abundance of clear evidence, may compel you to believe it, the way it is, somehow makes it easier to understand the actions of God, and perhaps makes Him seem a little more closely related to us humans and even more similar to us than we, possibly, would like.

Oh, I just want to complete something that I was talking about earlier, before I forget...if you recall, I previously mentioned the occasion where Jesus produced the fish in great abundance, and changed water into wine. Well, these "miracles" couldn't have happened without the transporter beam and spacecraft disguised behind the clouds, they simply beamed down a pile of previously captured fishes, and did the same thing with the wine/water. And again the same method was utilized in the multiplication of bread. Without the knowledge of the hidden spacecraft and its technological wonders, these "tricks" of course, would naturally appear to the masses to be nothing more than another of Jesus' great miracles.

I think it only normal though to question the superiority of any being that is proclaiming to be superior, and probably, it may even be considered good practice. Especially when you think of things like the time the poor and faithful fellow, who was commissioned by God to carry, and be the keeper and sole individual to look after a particular object for God, that he would not, at any time, open the contents of this sacred box in order to look inside, and reveal the contents to himself or anyone else. If, in fact, he took it upon himself to do such a thing, then he would as a consequence, be struck down, into death, by God himself.

I'm sure some of you will be familiar with this story. As the story goes, the faithful fellow is traveling with the sacred Ark of the Covenant, (see second Samuel verse 6 of the bible), in order that he may deliver it to the desired destination, and if I remember correctly, the wagon that carried the Ark rolled over a bump in the road or something and fell down causing the lid to fly off. Now he was faced with the problem of preparing it for transport again and during the process of trying to fix the situation, he did see and/or handle the actual contents of the sacred box, which is exactly what God had asked him to promise he would never do. Of course, God, being a man of his word, did cause the death of his faithful servant. However, I do believe that the contents of the sacred box were actually some sort of device that contained a lethal amount of radioactivity, and this was therefore the real reason that the man became ill and suddenly died. Of course he probably should not have been handling such dangerous materials without the appropriate attire equipped to protect him. However, I must say, that it is also entirely possible that Jehovah, again concealed from above by cloud cover, may have actually struck down the poor fellow on the spot, immediately with some kind of laser weapon within His holy space ship. It may therefore logically be considered also that Jehovah did kill him instantly, if indeed the Ark was radioactive, as an act of mercy in order to spare him the certain onslaught of a slow painful death due to the great toxic amount of radiation he would have suffered.

I sincerely hope that I have in no way at all caused any disillusionment with God by revealing these few well and long kept secrets; I merely intend to demystify our ancestors and relate just what I thoroughly believe. We not only have a right to a complete and unconditional understanding of our own religious "truths," but, these real explanations of Biblical events would not have even fallen into my hands if the creators had not wanted them to be revealed at this time. Therefore, in that light, one may even consider it a responsibility of any one of us, as brothers and sisters, to look out for each other, in any way we can, and help each other not only to survive, but to understand our own creators, and perhaps even forgive them if it is necessary, when we can. Therefore, in that family spirit of things, I would like to share those things that I have been fortunate enough to have had shared with me, in my confidence, as I was grateful for having been not only chosen, but also trusted to receive the information that I have. And as I consider it to be of great value, myself, I'm sure there are others that would be just as interested as I, and just as deserving, to be enlightened by the truth on these subjects. I sincerely hope that we can appreciate the knowledge for what it is, and in the spirit of an Avatar, share and use the information to the best of our abilities, and use these explanations offered by Jehovah, to come to a closer understanding of God, and perhaps even learn to accept Him differently, for the way He really is. It would be far too easy to be bitter or feel resentful after learning some of these truths, but I think it would also be far too childish. After all, let us not forget that this may be the brink of the last chance we may ever be able to receive any Divine intervention of any sort whatsoever. Do be careful here in your judgment of your God my friends, you may need Him more than you could possibly imagine. If this is so, then I will proceed to tell you of at least one very good reason for this necessity.

It has also been brought to my attention recently, that there is indeed a very serious potential threat looming on the horizon. Well, I suppose we still have just enough time to try to avoid it...if we believe the message and the messenger. I, for one, tend to trust my personal contact, and have every reason to and no reason not to. Nevertheless, I guess there will always be the positive ones amongst us, or the skeptical ones, that will argue that it won't happen, which is ok. In fact, I'm using all my personal powers of positive projection...probably, just in case there is any hope or truth of really avoiding such an ominous situation as the one I am about to describe to you.

CHAPTER 4

Divine Intervention

In approximately 180 years, there will most likely pass through our solar system, whether we like it or not, a very large supernova, or giant sun, which has come to the end of its hugeness and brilliance, and is in the process of dying, and like the superstar that it is, has decided to hurl itself through space on the way out, as if it is trying to take along with it as many planets, stars, and possibly suns that it can. And so it is that this giant burning sphere of light is heading directly toward the innocent and unsuspecting people of...you guessed it...planet Earth!

What a surprise for us, eh? I don't think too many of us suspected we might all go out in a great glorious blaze of fire, from a supernova. It was far more likely, I thought, that we would somehow be the cause of our own demise, rather than an act of God, but then it certainly wouldn't be the first time, would it? That is if you are a believer, if not, what the hell are you dong listening to my story? This is for believers only. Are you a spy perhaps? Well...we have ways of dealing with you.

Enough of that...back to the sad but probably true prediction for us here on Earth. I know that if that supernova is really going to be that close to us, we, the ever-existing people of Earth, will somehow struggle to overcome this ominous event, if it is possible. If not, we'll find an easier way to do it because we always do. I've personally calculated that there is actually just enough time (as if we had been tipped off just in the nick of time), to build ourselves enough flying crafts to carry every one of us to safety, just outside of our own inner galaxy, where Extraterrestrial scientists have predicted that this dying star is heading towards. Unfortunately, in order to do this, it may be necessary to build the crafts out of a certain type of very strong metal, which doesn't even exist here on this planet. However, it is very doubtful that anywhere within our own inner galaxy would be very safe from the enormous amount of heat that the supernova would generate during its "burnout" period of death. Coupled with the fact that the dying sun is already much larger than our own singular sun, I suspect that as it passes through our galaxy, on the way out, it will most likely have an enormous effect on all of the planets in our solar system, if it does not completely obliterate everything.

And so it seems we are facing inevitable doom, unless we are either saved by some divine intervention, or we take a huge leap of faith and endeavor to discover the type of metal that is needed to enable us high speed and great distance traveling. According to my sources, that particular type of metal is not to be found here on Earth, but it is to be available on the planet we call the moon. Yes that's right, our very own moon is going to save our ... well, let's not be hasty. In order to get to that metal, we will have to negotiate (further) with the Beings that are already mining that very same precious metal from our moon, for that very same reason. They need it to build their flying crafts as we do. Or if an agreement to share cannot be reached, we should consider the possibility that we might have to take it back by force. Somehow the former brainstorm of being saved by some divine intervention is beginning to sound better. Besides, who knows? Maybe there isn't enough of the metal to go around. There may only be enough to build enough crafts for half the people of Earth.

Well I always say, when you come to a fork in the road and cannot pick or choose one way over the other, it's probably best to make the time to go in both directions. It just may well be that is what it takes. It may be necessary to go in both directions in order for all to succeed, if you know what I mean. For instance: if I was unsure of any positive rescue effort, or maybe there just isn't enough room for all of us to expect to be rescued, it makes sense to cover all possibilities and ensure safety for continuance of the species, then we should endeavor to create two or three plans, if we really want to accommodate everyone, which doesn't always seem to be obvious ... especially if you consider what I am about to explain.

A few decades ago the United States government did have what they thought was just cause and reason to engage and enter into a contract with a certain group of aliens that we call the "Grays." The important and specific terms of the agreement between the groups were as follows: the U.S. government was, and still is, to allow the Aliens, or Grays, to continue to perform their experiments here on Earth, specifically in the U.S., and they would be allowed to continue these experiments in exchange for some technical information on building and designing flying crafts. Of course the information was, and still is, more advanced than any other kind of information available on Earth.

It was that particular information that has made it possible for the existence and creation of what is know as the Stealth bomber and Stealth technology. With the advanced information of the Grays, and with their cooperation, the U.S. government was able to construct an original craft with some kind of hidden and secret method of propulsion. That is to say that the real driving force behind the machine is concealed and it in fact carries two conventional jet engine housings on it so as to deceive the onlooker. So, in a way, one could say that the Grays have indeed helped to save us from 'sudden insanity'[9] during the Gulf War and Desert Storm.

The dealings with the Grays are not entirely as smooth as all this might have you believing. Just before I tell you of another extraordinary encounter that occurred with the Grays, I will enforce that statement with more detailed information concerning that same government/ Gray contract. Indeed there is justification for questioning the kind of experiments that the Grays are engaged in. You have most likely already heard about the disappearing cattle all over the United States, and even the mysterious mutilated and unknown numbers of cows that have been discovered lying in pastures. If not, you have heard now. And I can say without a doubt that these missing and mutilated cattle are the end result of experiments that the Grays have been involved in. You might find that this is not too surprising, but I'm sure you'll

---

[9] Suddam Hussien

be shocked when you discover that the U.S. government is not only standing by, watching and doing nothing in order to honor their part of the contract, but the government is also powerless to do anything about the human abductions that the Grays are involved in, according to the terms of their agreement. Believe it or not, it's really happening!

I should also say, on behalf of the government that they seem to be having second thoughts about the whole affair. I'm also quite sure that they are considering it one of the biggest mistakes they have ever made. Naturally the government is terrified of telling its faithful and understanding merry band of citizens, or they would have said something by now. What I think is most important is that they begin to trust the civilians at least as much as they have entrusted them, and secondly they must lose all their fear of dealing with the matter in an open and honest way; they must seek the support of their dear people in order to overcome this problem. Perhaps, on the optimistic side of things, all this will bring them all together, and strengthen their relationship. Third, and perhaps most important of all, they should probably pray to their God and Creator for help…and believe that He already knows about the Grays and their secret contracts, just as He knows about the level of classification of a secret document actually being a higher classification that a top secret document is in Federal agencies.

But that's not all folks; it gets scarier yet! Yep, you must certainly have asked yourself the question, what are all these abductions and mutilations about? Well, let's start with the cattle ranchers have been finding dead in their fields, with no tire tracks or footprints that lead either to or from the cold and stiff carcasses. Besides the unknown DNA experiments they might be performing, the Grays have to eat, or should I say, they need nutrition too. As it is known that they have been around for a very long time, not the longest though, and during the course of their genetic evolution, they have somehow developed beyond the ability to eat and chew. In fact, they have only a little slit where their mouths once were, and no longer can they open it wide enough to put any solid food into.

Apparently they have found a way to overcome this little problem. What they do is mix their protein (in this case cattle, but they are also known to be cannibalistic) with some kind of acidic solution that is similar to sulphuric acid. This turns the meat and everything into a mushy substance, which can then be rubbed onto the surface of their gray colored skin, and absorbed into the body through the process of osmosis. And, as if that isn't strange enough, wait till I tell you how they reproduce! But first I must say that these Grays, so called after the color of their skin, are to be avoided at all costs for not only are they cannibalistic, but they have a nasty habit of enslaving us humans to do their heavy manual labor. Which is strange in itself, because, for the most part, they tend to be stronger that the average human from this planet. In fact, they have superhuman strength and it is wise not to try armwrestling with them. But here is one comforting thought: they can be killed with a knife or a gun, etc., but one should never stare directly into their eyes as they have the ability to hypnotize you like that. So once they've captured their innocent and unsuspecting victim, possibly by disguising themselves and their craft, coming in the guise of an angel or messenger from God, as they are clever little devils and have the ability to look very convincing in their disguises and could fool any inexperienced person ... anyway, let's consider the poor people that were unlucky enough to have already been captured. Once they have successfully made off with their victim, they can then, among other things, drug him and turn him into a relative zombie slave and take him away to the moon for the specific slave duty of mining for the precious metal that they need to build their spaceships. Let's hope they don't clean us out completely as that may be the only hope for some of us Earthlings.

I suppose once the zombieslave has outgrown his usefulness, they have the option of eating or "absorbing" him as dinner. Well I for one am all for termination of that same contract which the U.S. government has with the Grays, and am quite sure of their feeling of regret for even getting involved with them in the first place. But then I'm a Canadian, so what does it really matter what I might be thinking about anything anyway? Well just in case it does matter, I'm going to tell you the rest of what I know about the Grays. As a matter of fact, not all of them look exactly alike. Some of them have taken on the disguise of being human and look just like the rest of us. Some of them even look like children, but are actually much stronger than a full-grown man. Other Grays stand taller than most of us humans and again, they all seem to be stronger than us. They also have a strange and nasty habit of appearing from seemingly out of nowhere by entering into your house through the walls or the roof. Uh…certainly not the kind of characters that one should take lightly, in fact, I think it's safe to say that it's not really safe within their presence.

Now I'd like to tell you about the ridiculous but ingenious method of regeneration of their species. It would seem, according to the story, that these odd creatures actually and literally grow their own kind on a mixture of the remnants of their foodstuffs (whether it be human remains or animal) and that acidic substance that I told you about earlier. Somehow they have a method of planting their own DNA into the mushy substance and it develops and grows out of that process, henceforth, reproduction of the species. I should mention that they are trying to change the way they reproduce and the way they consume nutrition by cross-breeding their species with ours, to their credit, hence the abductions of earth females and subsequent impregnation.

Well, I hope that's all I have to tell you about the Grays. I think I'd like to move onto the next subject, except to say that it is equally important for the citizens of the U.S. to encourage their own government to not be afraid to overcome their problems with the Grays and perhaps even say a prayer as well. I'm quite confident that if they all band together, and believe, they can surpass their difficulties in this and any other situation.

The other incident that seems to have involved the presence and influence of the Grays, although the only real clue I have that indicates them, is the type of craft that was encountered during this amazing adventure, or a least, a small, but very significant part of the entire adventure, an adventure that is so fantastic that it is difficult to believe that it really took place. This portion of the adventure is about a specific number of events in the life of a man that goes by the name of Buzz Andrews.

CHAPTER 5

Buzz Andrews

It's been quite a while since I was able to read about his adventures in a document that was provided for my information by a friend, about the past adventures of a fellow called Buzz (not to be confused with the famous Buzz Aldren, who was also an astronaut). Anyway, our story, should you choose to believe it, is about this other Buzz character, and as I read it from a CIA classified "Top Secret" document, (which, as I said before, is not as high as the classification "Secret"). He was a man who at one time during his life had a very deep desire to fly, as he was a pilot himself, in the kind of crafts that we call UFOs. He also longed for some kind of adventure with God that could somehow answer all of his questions, or a least some of them.

I've only read part 1 of this 2 part story... which I also remember as being an autobiography, or confessions of an exCIA agent. I am still hoping to be able to read part 2 as well. Again, it's been a while since I saw that story, and they're not easy to find, so I hope to wipe away the clouds from the foggy memory of it all as I tell it to you. Even though there are great numbers of events that happen, I feel it is necessary to relate to you as much of it as I can remember, in order that you can grasp the entire situation, or context, that surround our 'hero' in this little tale.

I've just spent quite a bit of time telling you of certain Earth/ Extraterrestrial encounters from some very distant times gone by, so it may intrigue your imagination a little bit more to hear the events I'm about to relate to you concerning these more recent times gone by, more specifically the story of Buzz Andrews. Although he worked for the CIA as an adult, it would seem that he spent a lot of his years as a young man going around and entering into or joining several different groups of communal style people, and I think even some either religious or satanic kinds of cults as well. Most of the infiltration into these communes was confined to the more simple communal style living and sharing everything kinds of folks that could possibly and naturally consist of very similar religious principles. Now of course in his own, but not singular, redneck way of thinking, each and every one of those no good, long hair, anti Christian, lazy, freaky bums, were all considered to be, in his opinion, not worthy of living. And so therefore, he and his buddies went around invading the privacy of these folks, yelling and screaming at them, and beating on them, and in general trying to disband them and send them all home. I'm sure many of the beatings were professionally done, as Buzz himself, and I don't know how many of his other buddies, were trained in the practice of the Martial Arts (you know – Kung Fu, kick boxing, etc.) It was sometime after this period that his amazing adventure began. It's as if God himself had heard his prayers and he was possibly going to be rewarded somehow for all his efforts to stamp out the pacifists with his fascist friends. But somehow, he, out of all of them he had worked with, had been picked out of many to go on the strangest journey and experience the most fantastic adventures ... perhaps he would even have his dream come true and one day learn to and actually be able to fly all by himself in an unidentified flying saucer, or some unknown but fantastically technically advanced flying machine.

Yes, indeed, it would seem that God would in fact, 'reward' Buzz for all his hard work. However, God had a very different kind of reward in mind. In fact, He wanted to give Buzz an adventure that he would never forget, and so He designed a special, personalized adventure that would hopefully teach Buzz the errors of his ways, as this special adventure God had in mind for him had been designed to give Buzz a nice helping of the excitement that he so loved, or at least seemed to enjoy and thrive upon. Although there was plenty of room left in the basic design of the adventure for Buzz himself to design a little of the adventure personally. And so he did, as if he wasn't going to be having enough fun and excitement as it was.

In the beginning of the journey the original contact was made as Buzz was driving down a remote highway somewhere on the west coast of the U.S.A., most likely California. As he was going along right in the midst of all the fog and rain of the evening, he suddenly lost control of the functions of his vehicle, and went sliding out of control and off the roadway, only to come to a miraculous screeching halt, just off the roadside, leaving a trail of burned rubber.

The only remote clue that was apparent, left to toy with his terror of the moment was a bluish beam of light that came streaming down out of the sky which drenched him and his vehicle in the light, and obviously seizing control of the vehicle from him, forcing him off the road, he barely came to a safe stop on the roadside. So Buzz is "contacted." Thus begins Buzz's wonderful adventure introducing a couple of characters that "happened" to be coming down the road just behind him witnessing his strange accident that happened as a result of extreme loss of control over the vehicle. In fact, the vehicle itself seemed to lose control of its own functions, that is, by some mysterious but outside force, all normal and functioning parts suddenly seized as if something had instantly frozen everything: steering, brakes, etc. Again mysteriously, and might I say miraculously, nevertheless, he was somehow able to come to a safe stop at the side of the road, only to sit there in shock, and try to come to some sort of understanding of what had just happened to him.

It was some time after that when the two men who were just behind him on the highway approached him. It was raining that evening, so the accident looked normal enough if you were to consider that he was merely hydroplaning. However, Buzz wasn't looking on the accident as an observer, but as a participant, and from where he sat, this was not, in any way, a normal accident. Far from it, he thought, as he opened his window to greet the strangers now banging on his window for the second time, trying to release him from his posttraumatic trancelike state.

"Are you okay?" asked one of the strangers, who had obviously come to see if Buzz was indeed okay. There was a short pause until the other man, who looked very much like a Native American Indian, even in the dim moonlight, repeated the same question again, asking Buzz if he was okay, just as if they really cared about him. Somehow Buzz had to figure there was something unusual about that, probably from lack of numerous caring experiences. He found that it was slightly disturbing to have someone adamantly trying to reach out and contact him. At any rate, he decided to snap out of it and roll down the window to let them know that he was okay, or a least he was okay until now, at which point he became slightly agitated about the fact that he had absolutely no idea what had just happened to his vehicle, and was unsure if he would be able to get it running again.

Suddenly he realized that this person who he would ordinarily consider to be, to say the least, a minority figure in his mind, might just be very important to him in the next little while, and so it occurred to him that he should probably try to seem friendly towards them both. I'm sure that you will be just as shocked as I was to find out that there is a rather sardonic but fitting end to the entire adventure. I mean, who would have thought that such a radical and faithfully devoted straight up redneck sort of fellow such as Buzz would end up being not only friends with the two unlikely companions, but actually develop real caring feeling for the Indian and his friend. The truly remarkable and unforeseen, shocking irony of the situation is that he, Buzz Andrews, would actually share in the sacrificial burning and inhaling of a marijuana reefer with his two, newly discovered associates. Although I'm 100% sure right now that if you were to tell him that at the time, he would not only doubt it completely, the old Buzz Andrews would probably punch any other hippy type right in the nose for even suggesting such a ridiculous idea.

But that was the 'old' Buzz, and these hippy types were the only people around right now on an otherwise deserted and secluded stretch of the road. Besides that, Buzz felt somewhere deep inside him that these two strangers had a more than passing role to play in the game of his life, and so for these reasons he figured he had better appear unprejudiced and, furthermore, downright friendly. And so he did just that, opening the door to get out of his vehicle, before it decided to do something else again, all by itself.

After standing there talking to the two men for a little bit, they all decided that they had definitely seen a bluish colored light shining down out of the sky above them, and it shone directly onto Buzz's vehicle. Somehow, somebody had forced him off the road by taking control of his vehicle and brought him to a stop. Needless to say, the whole experience raised a few questions in his mind. Like who was responsible? And why were they doing that to him? Well, Buzz didn't know it yet but the two strangers that he was now riding with, three abreast in their pickup truck to the nearest gas station to find a tow truck, had answers to both of his questions, and a lot more as well.

They had traveled some distance now, and still no sign of any means of getting help, not even a phone. Suddenly the driver of the truck slowed down and turned the vehicle around, saying, "I'll bet if you went back and tried it now, it would start up and everything would be just fine." Now how can you be sure of that? Buzz wondered. The two fellows went on to explain the reason his truck went off the road and, as well as knowing who he was, they were also aware of his great desire to experience traveling in an extraterrestrial craft, and that if he was indeed serious about it, they were there to make the necessary arrangements. Buzz could not believe what he was hearing. He thought they were joking, and felt slightly irritated that his deepest and most privately secret thoughts had been somehow invaded.

"You've got to be kidding!" Buzz exclaimed.

"No, Mr. Andrews, we're quite serious."

By the time they returned to where his vehicle was sitting, safely by the side of the road, they almost had him convinced that they were for real and meant every word they said about taking him up for a ride in their craft. But Buzz was somehow not quite convinced that all they were saying was true.

"Look, go and get back into your vehicle, start it up, and be on your way then, but think about what we've told you seriously, and should you have a change of heart, well, we'll check on you in a couple of days, in case you change your mind." With that, they left him at his vehicle, assuring him that it would work just fine, and they were off again back into nowhere, just as quickly as they came.

He just stood there, quite dazed for a moment, wondering as he stared into the empty distance, how they knew what they knew and that his vehicle would really work again, thinking that if he could start it, that might just mean everything else they were talking about could be true also. They were right. It started. No longer upset or angry over the whole situation, he drove away, curiously pleased with himself, and continued on in a semi trancelike state, dreaming about what it would be like to actually travel through the different galaxies of the universe.

Much to his surprise, he would need that journey through space far more than he could possibly realize. For within the short space of the next few days, Buzz would find himself in more trouble than he could possibly desire. It would seem that there was more than one group of interested individuals watching over him. However, the second group of people to contact him was of the kind that didn't have his best interests in mind. Now as far as I can surmise, the only real reason that the "bad guys" could have for wanting Buzz dead...or on their side, is that they must have been afraid of him as a foe. Whatever their reason, it was enough to motivate them to pay Buzz a little visit, and I don't mean a very friendly visit either.

Somehow the forces of evil had become aware of his recent interest in space travel, and again, I say that there must be a reason for their fear of Buzz. Whatever they were afraid of was enough to want him out of the way.

Of course, he never suspected that his innocent curiosity would have ever been enough to get him killed! He was about to find out just how dead they actually wanted him. Again, on some lonely area of the roadway, he found himself trapped, if you will, by a couple of other vehicles, and even a helicopter! He could no longer drive, and before he could grasp the gravity of the situation, he found himself staring down the barrel of a very scary bazooka!

CHAPTER 6

The Beginning of Buzz's Extreme Adventures

These characters meant serious business. They weren't about to even give him a chance to talk his way out of…whatever it is that they were so upset about, which in my opinion, is very rude and tacky. I mean almost everyone deserves at least one chance to make a change. In reality though, these Men in Black (MIB) have much less than even a first chance in mind for anybody unlucky enough to be left to their mercy.

If I can muster the courage to tell y'all about what they really do have planned for certain individuals then you may find it easier to understand their next action toward Buzz. Before he could even speak, the dark figure of a man that was holding the bazooka pulled the trigger and fired the thing directly at Buzz Andrews! He had about enough time to think to himself, "This is it, I'm going to die." Well how many of you guessed it? There's one way that he could have escaped that situation and, lucky him, he found it. Even as he watched the flames leaping out of the bazooka, another kind of flash of light came down from above him, again like before, a similar blue beam engulfed him and the next think he knew, he was sitting staring out of a window and flying at a very rapid speed out over the water.

That is, in the blink of an eye, literally, he had gone from sure death in front of the bazooka, instantly beamed up, and was some great distance out over the water, and traveling very quickly in what appeared to be some sort of single occupant flying saucer. What's more, he had absolutely no idea who or what was piloting the craft. One thing he was sure of though, and that is that he could see that he was traveling very fast, further out over the ocean. He was also sure that somehow, the craft he was in was indeed being piloted, or controlled by someone, but who, and from where? Well he would soon find out, but for the moment, there was something more interesting to turn his attention to. Way down below, on the surface of the water, he could see, clearly, three or four ships were cruising through the water, and he could see the wake left trailing behind them. Then he saw what looked like Japanese flags waving from the decks of the ships. In another blink of an eye, the ships started to fire at Buzz and his craft, and amazingly, the craft started to swoop and sway out of the direct line of fire! After very deliberately avoiding several unprovoked shots from the ship's cannons, the craft sped up an increased altitude in order to be out of the firing range of the cruisers. Below him he could see the various different shaped islands and larger landmasses until he came upon a huge mountain range.

As if flown by an expert pilot, they glided safely into an open area in the mountain and came to a safe, soft stop on a level surface there, and he climbed down out of the precision flying machine that brought him to this secret mountain hideout. As he climbed down from the machine, he could see three or four individuals some distance from where he was, walking towards him, and so he began to walk towards them to greet his new comrades. As they got closer to him he began to recognize two of the men as the two men that he, "ran into" the night on the highway when he was forced off the road. As they got closer, he could make out the features of the Indian looking fellow and his companion, who also had a fairly dark complexion, but he almost looked like he might be from the Middle East, probably Greece, but it was hard to really define the exact accent that he spoke with.

So the men chatted for a while about what had just transpired, and took Buzz into a cave nearby and explained how they had just saved him in the nick of time, and of course he was extremely grateful that they had. What he had actually been flying in was what is known as a scout ship, which is usually flown automatically that is, unmanned, but they can also carry at least one passenger. It can be remotely controlled, from the Mother ship, and there are a least three or four different kinds of power that drive and propel them.

They went on to explain that in many of the major mountain ranges like the one they were on now, in the Himalayas, the ETs have secret hideouts. As well, they've been there for hundreds of years. From there, they went on to say that they would love to take Buzz along with them for an intergalactic journey on their Mother ship. With one quick thought to recall just exactly what was waiting for him back home, Buzz decided instantly that he could not afford to pass up their invitation.

In order for the Mother ship to pick them up, it is necessary that the individual about to be beamed up have the strength and presence of mind so that the transportation of the person is completed safely. There is no room for doubt or anxiety at all. One must be confident and relaxed, and in no way nervous at all because the wrong state of mind could actually be fatal! However, Buzz had already had his initiation, and felt just that much more confident, for having already gone through it once, even though he really had no time to become afraid or anxious before, as I said, it all happened in the blink of an eye.

So it wasn't long before they found themselves aboard the huge craft they call the Mother ship, and it is precisely this kind of craft that is used for intergalactic traveling. Of course they wanted to give their guest a tour of the ship once he was aboard, and it all began in the lounge, I guess you'd call it, where they could all have a drink, and chat a bit, over a nice alcoholic beverage. They wanted Buzz to feel as comfortable as possible. He didn't know it yet, but according to his God, they still had a little surprise waiting for him, but that could wait…or could it? Buzz raised his glass to tilt his drink and noticed a very beautiful woman enter the lounge area where they were drinking… (perhaps this was the surprise).

After getting acquainted with each other briefly, Buzz and his new companion decided to go for a walk around the ship a little, as she was going to be his official tour guide. She showed him many interesting things that were all very new concepts entirely, like the special little room they have that couples can enter into and connect with each other with the help of a certain machine, that works in connection with the couple's simultaneous back to back meditation, operated by helmets that they each wear, and their thoughts. It can be very helpful and useful in order to bring the couple closer together and strengthen what they already have between them. They did that together and apparently it is quite exhilarating, and is something that I'm sure all couples would benefit from and should love to try.

She asked him if time was going to be an object or problem with him, because she wanted to know just how long he would be able to stay with them. Again, with one quick reflection, he knew instantly what he wanted to do. He didn't care if he ever returned to Earth, all that he wanted to do now was stay with his new friend as long as possible and experience as many new things as he could. As far as he could tell, he was falling deeply in love with this beautiful woman and her rather dark olive complexion and long dark hair. So that settled it for him, and with that they were off, to complete the tour and his introduction to the spacecraft. She began to show him all kinds of wonderful things like the way in which they can bathe, and do some laundry all at once. Simply by stepping into a little room that bathes the occupant in some kind of intense white light, and that's it, you step out of the room and you're clean again, and so is everything that you're wearing! Good for another day, or whatever.

Anyway, there they are, falling in love with each other, living in a dream world, walking around the ship, and as she was showing him all the interesting stuff aboard the craft, they came upon the place, I believe near the centre of the ship, that is very much like a terrarium, that of course had a very bright light like sunlight, only it wasn't. Everywhere he looked he could see all kinds of tropical looking plants and beautifully colored birds, etc. As he marveled at the amazing, wondrous sights before him, he took a few steps into the room ahead of his new friend Debbie and walked towards a small cliff directly in front of him, and suddenly, over the crest of the cliff appeared a very large tiger! Of course Buzz was surprised as hell to be greeted by such a ferocious beast in the middle of all this peacefulness. He wondered if perhaps it could have been a tame tiger.

At that moment, Debbie screamed at him to be careful not to get too close to it, but before he could even react, almost before she finished her sentence, the tiger pounced off the cliff and leaped with graceful ease, right directly onto poor Mr. Andrews! This he did not expect to happen. And for another split-second, he remembered facing the bazooka and that intense sinking feeling, like his body was about to go down for the last time, while the spirit heads in another direction. He really thought that was going to be the end of him, and he cursed himself aloud as he realized that he was reaching for an empty knife case. He had handed it over to them as he first came aboard the ship, at their request, just until they felt they could trust him a little more. And with that, the full force of the roaring tiger in flight came thundering down and crashed upon him, forcing Buzz to fall onto his back with the now even larger looking beast right on top of him. He could hear his new girlfriend screaming in the background as the tiger's razor sharp claws raked into his shoulder and sides, and he couldn't believe that the tiger was actually beginning to open his enormous jaws, revealing the ugliest and scariest mouth he had ever stared at, like it was getting ready to clamp down on his head, and finish him off! This was enough to cause Buzz to remember all of the nasty deeds he'd committed in his past, as his life, flashed before his eyes. Even as he felt the hot breath of the tiger closing in on him and filling his gasping nostrils with whiffs of stinky bloody tiger breath he wondered if he had ever really scared anybody that much, or hurt anyone bad enough to have deserved this attack from out of the blue. Although he felt that he did not deserve to die yet, and especially in such an awful manner, he just gave up the fight, as the effort was completely futile at this point.

Just as he closed his eyes for what he thought would be the last time, and squeezed them shut as tightly as he could as if it would help shut out the pain as the tiger bit into his neck and head, the huge and heavy beast let out a sickening painful cry and collapsed like a puppet with its strings cut, dropping it's entire bulk of deadweight on top of Buzz, causing his breath to be pushed out of him…again he couldn't believe what was happening to him, and had to open and close his eyes a couple of times just to clear his head of doubt. Yeah, he was wide awake, adrenalin pumping, heart racing, and everything was real and still as it was, so, he concluded, this must be real.

As he began to relax a bit, he became more aware of the pain in his wounds. At that moment, all the people that were in the area, a half dozen or so, came rushing over to his side to assist him by pulling the tiger off of him and helping him get out from underneath. Everyone fussed over him and asked if he was strong enough to walk to the medical treatment room, and he thought he could make it with a little supervision, so off they went, with his girlfriend under his left arm, and another stranger on his right side, supporting him as they walked. Sensing that he was probably in shock, Debbie began to say reassuring things to him, and tried to comfort him to calm him down. Only now did his mind begin to clear up enough so that he could realize that he still didn't know exactly what had happened!

"How did I get out of that with my life?" he asked. One of the other witnesses indicated that he had his companion to thank for that. He looked at her, the expressions on his face indicating that he was about to repeat the question. Before he could though, she had already anticipated what he was going to say, (read his mind), and began to speak up and answer him.

"Well…I've got something to tell you," she confessed. "That whole tiger episode was planned right from the beginning, and I must say," she continued, "that it all went down quite perfectly, I'm sure you couldn't have done it better even if you had practiced it over and over. Please don't be offended, I wasn't in favor of the idea you know, but I've got my orders from the top too, and I was really only doing what was asked of me by my superiors. I really didn't like the idea from the beginning and I became more opposed to it, as I got closer to you. I hope you're not angry with me, and our medical team will have those wounds of yours all fixed up in no time at all." By now they had reached the room where the medical facilities were located, and she helped him onto a sort of stretcher or bed and waved the doctor over to his side.

"Angry?" Buzz exclaimed, "I'm still a little confused about it all, but you're friend said that I should thank you for escaping the tiger attack with my life."

Well, it is true," she said, "if I had not known about the tiger, I'm sure that it would have taken us both by surprise." She moved over a little so as to let the doctor get in close and begin the very strange treatment. "But, I did know about it all and that's why I fell behind you a bit and kept myself a safe distance from the beast," she reached into her 'holster' and took out her personal weapon in order to explain in detail, "so that when it attacked you, I would be ready for it." Showing him the 'ray gun', she continued, "I'm really sorry I didn't shoot at it sooner, and in any other situation, I would have, but, as I said, I've got my orders to follow."

"You're still responsible for saving me Debbie," he said, "and I believe you when you say you had no choice. I do mean it when I say thank you, my dear, but tell me more about that weapon of yours, can you tell me how it works, and why it is so quiet? I didn't hear a thing."

"Thanks for believing me, and I want you to know that there won't be any more surprises in store for you, well nothing unpleasant anyway," she leaned over and kissed him lusciously on the lips for a few seconds, retracted herself and gave him a lovely warm smile that seemed to say, 'don't worry, you can trust me completely.' "I think that little session we had together in the 'couples' chamber may have done you some good," she stated. He agreed, as he did notice a bit of change in his verbal manner. He felt more open and trusting, willing to share the feeling in his heart, which is exactly what the chamber is supposed to accomplish, among other things.

But please, tell me how that thing works." He pleaded as he pointed at her strange looking weapon.

So she went on to explain that what she had was a hand-held weapon, or 'ray gun', that actually shoots a beam or ray of intense light, like a typical laser beam. However, it has the ability, and is capable of directing three laser beams of different intensity. The first beam, like all the rest, is identified by the color, which indicates the exact type of laser that it is. In order to change from one beam to the next, the user simply increases the pressure that had been applied onto the trigger. So upon squeezing the trigger, the very first ray that comes forth from it is green in color, and is actually used to promote healing. Much like the one the doctor used on his cuts and wounds the tiger ripped into his flesh. So the first ray that is produced from the gun is used to heal, and not to hurt. The second ray that is produced simply by increasing the trigger pressure a little bit is actually blue in color, and surprisingly, doesn't really hurt the victim either, but it will render a person unconscious for a little while, exactly just how long, I don't really know. I'm sure it is a very effective method of taking control of a bad situation, without harming the person in any way. If, however, it becomes necessary to kill you're opponent, well this cute little weapon can do that, also. Again, simply by increasing the trigger pressure a third time, the laser ray changes color and intensity again, and the beam that is produced this time is red in color. It is very deadly, and will kill any human that you aim it at. Of course it would also kill animals, obviously, but it wasn't necessary to kill the tiger so she only stunned it and knocked it out for a short time. This is something she would have learned to do as a child because they even have an exact replica of the ray gun, only it is a toy that is used by the children during playing 'guns'. In a way, it does sort of teach them and prepare them for when they are all grown up and ready to use a real laser gun, because it changes color as well, and in the very same manner as the real one.

Of course, that is only one of, who knows how many, different types of weapons that are out there, in the different galaxies. I'd like to interrupt this little tale of the adventures of Mr. Buzz, for just a short moment in order to tell you about another type of weapon, that I've learned about. It is a weapon that was invented by the Pleiadians…or at least it is one that they presently have and use. This particular type of laser gun is, to say the least, incredibly amazing, and I'm quite sure that there are those sorts of creatures alive today, even on this planet, that would do absolutely anything in order to get their paws on one of these. I must admit, that it is indeed an ultimately desirable weapon. Naturally, I would hope to never really have to use it, or need it, but it would sure be handy if I ever needed to feel that safe. Enough praise already, ok, I'll get on with the details.

You may or may not have already heard of a fellow named Billy Meirs, well his personal E.T. contact is well documented on video tape, at least, anyway, and it is thanks indeed to him for his personal testimony to his amazing eye witness accounts of the famous and elusive Pleiadian craft and it's occupants! Again, his amateur video recordings of many difficult and impressive maneuvers, only help to do nothing but secure a verdict of authenticity surrounding all of the information that he has so graciously and selflessly decided to try and share with the world, and what does he get for it? Shot at a half a dozen times, and this to include several very near misses, the old shot in the book in the pocket story. If the woman had not have been so inexperienced with the proper use and discharge of a firearm, Billy would surely be dead by now. She later apologized and is now an avid E.T. buff, not to mention a personal student of the man she once tried to kill. Thank God she did not succeed in silencing this man. One thing that we have learned from him is that the Pleiadian people certainly take their discharge of firearms seriously. Not only do they have exact replicas of the real thing for their kids to play and practice with, but the real thing is very impressive indeed.

This particular weapon that I am about to describe to you is also very impressive. Let's say that the target you were to pick just in order to test the efficiency of this gun was a tree. Only this tree can be anywhere, a distance of up to and not more than 36kms from where you're standing. Next you aim the laser gun in the exact general direction of the tree, look down at a visual monitor screen that is on the gun, and as you think of the exact likeness of the tree, the picture on the gun monitor matches you're thought, and shows up on the screen so you can see your target, even if it is out of visual range to the naked eye. You simply pull the trigger and it let's out a very intense laser beam burning everything in it's path and causing that part of the tree that you wish to focus on to simply disappear, whether it be a large part of the tree, or just a particular leaf on a particular branch. Of course it isn't necessary to shoot it through everything that is in the general path of you're intended target. But, it's also nice to know that you can if you want to. The laser beam is so powerful that it will cause everything that it touches to disappear.

Then again, there is also the kind of healing laser beam, like the one they used on Buzz. They merely aim the healing ray of light at his wounds, caused by the tiger with his claws, and bathe the lacerated area with the healing green light form the laser beam and the wounds seal up instantly, completely disinfected, and the flesh returns to normal!

Well lucky for Buzz, at least that's how he felt when they healed over his wounds, and quite grateful as well, but he couldn't help but wonder if anything like that might happen again. He wasn't sure if an incident like that served to strengthen the relationship between Debbie and him, or weaken it. He supposed that too many incidents like that wouldn't be too good. But that there probably was a reason for it, and maybe he even deserved it. He reflected on his past, and some of the hippie communes that he had paid a 'visit' to.

Enough of that, he thought, back into his waking dream that involved this olive skinned beauty and her strange surroundings.

Over the period of the next few weeks they planned sort of a tour of the galaxies, some of the different planets and their occupants, and the rest of the spaceship, which itself had an odd assortment and collection of some of the different species that they have encountered in their travels. And I might add some very strange species of beings indeed!

One particular group of these weird creatures they befriended consisted of a Praying Mantis like creature. These ones, they had aboard the craft with them. These grotesque looking things were actually quite intelligent and they communicated by means of mental telepathy. Another of these odd beings they had encountered in their travels consisted of a bunch of rocklike creatures! Yeah, that's what I said… they look like huge boulders or rocks, kind of round in shape, with no exposed features that would indicate that it was anything other than a rock, but they also have the ability to communicate via telepathic waves. These particular beings are especially noted for their ability to empathize. Just exactly what they are made of, I'm not quite sure, but it would seem that they are not only creatures of great conscience, but they appear to have the characteristics of having huge hearts as well. If I remember correctly, they do eat and can move, however very slowly, so that they must crawl on top of their intended meal of vegetation, and sort of absorb their meal through the process of osmosis. These particular creatures they had to visit on their home world planet and so they traveled the few short light years to their native land in order to experience them. As they talked to them and listened to what they had to say, they learned that they were the kind of beings that for some reason seemed to care a great deal for the well-being of others, in that capacity they encouraged individuals to do the things they really enjoyed the most. They also expressed a great desire to play hockey. Although they themselves were not physically able to do it, they wished that they could.

Well, as if these, crazy encounters weren't strange enough in themselves; they would at least serve to prepare him, if that's possible, for what adventures lay ahead for him. The entire succession of events would, to say the least, leave Buzz with a desire and hunger to return to a reality that he was a little more used to. But, before he would relieve that hunger for a more familiar environment, he would most certainly encounter some even more confusing circumstances. Next, it seems, he was to learn to pilot his own craft! Where it would take him, was really anyone's guess. The privilege of piloting one's own craft, can also open doors to very distant destinations, and offer certain freedoms and an individual control over one's own destiny, if you so desire. But it is also wise, as in any adventure and most advisable for one to always chart, whenever possible, the intended course or at least provide somebody at home base with a map of where you intend to be exploring especially if it's going to be new or previously uncharted territory, just in case something goes wrong or you don't return on time. There are places out there that are more difficult to return from than others.

This was the type of place that Mr. Andrews was about to discover. But first, he would need to know just how to get there. Whether or not anyone had actually intended that he should discover this place or not, I wonder…as he himself would soon wonder.

CHAPTER 7

Nirvana or Buzz Learns to Fly

So this brings us back to the time where he is given the freedom of flight. The time where Buzz Andrews begins his initial training, and this time he gets to not only fly alone, but actually pilot the craft as well, and therefore obtain the ability to go just wherever it pleases him. The time is taken to carefully show Buzz just exactly everything that he needs to know in order to control a single occupant craft, and how to take him, and this craft wherever he should like to go. And this training would include specific instructions on how to go through "windows". This phenomenon called a "window" occurs commonly between one dimension, and another. The passage way, or door which we call a window, is precisely just that, and acts just as you might suspect, as a portal, or means of getting from one particular dimension, to another. But we must be careful that the vessel used to transport us between the dimensions, and through the window, is constructed of a very strong kind of material. Usually a type of metal, not found here on Earth. The forces at play inside the window are very powerful and could easily crush the wrong material.

Just to give you an example of a window, we have one, at least, here on Earth. I'm sure everyone's heard of it by now. We know it here on Earth by the name, the Bermuda Triangle. There is, in fact, a window that exists within the location of the Bermuda Triangle that can quickly take you from one dimension to another. But I'll get to that destination later, for now, let's get back to the adventures of Buzz, as he is about to go through a window, a different one, one that will take him to a place that would be considered peaceful, if we could compare it to the window of the Triangle, or at least what we have come to discover to be true about the window of the Bermuda Triangle, and what is on the other side of the window, or what we have discovered to be there so far, anyway. Who knows, perhaps the window could lead to more than one place. The "windows" seem to have similarities to what we call black holes. Similarities in that, they both have the ability to crush anything that enters into them that happens to be weak enough. It's difficult to measure or even guess just exactly how strong the object must be in order to survive going through one of these without being crushed, and I can give you an example of the reason it's so hard to say.

If I were to tell you that I know of a story of someone going through a black hole and surviving, with nothing other than the skin on his back and his skeletal structure and other flesh and blood body parts, would you believe me?

Perhaps that story would be more believable if I tell you the rest of it. Yes it's true, the being did survive the first black hole, but it was the second one that killed him. Now I don't know the exact size of the holes or the difference in size relativity, of one to the other, it's even possible that being the same size, hypothetically, one could still be stronger than the other. What I do know about this to be the truth is that the being involved was not what you may think of as you're normal human being, in fact he was quite exactly like an ordinary man from the head down to his waist, but after that, well let's just say, have ya'll ever heard of a Centaur? Well if you haven't, which I doubt, but just in case, I'll tell you, that a Centaur is actually half a man, and half a horse, all joined at the hips and shoulders, so that the result is a four legged creature with the torso and head of a man! Put that in your pipe and smoke it!

Now, as history would have it, this was no ordinary Centaur, no indeed, this Centaur was the captain of his own spacecraft. At the time of the accident the captain was riding in the observation deck on top of the craft, which was encased over with a transparent bubble like shield, but there was a 'malfunction' in the observation "bubble", and the invisible force field dematerialized and the poor captain was sucked out into space and was consequently sucked right into a black hole, but miraculously, he lived through the ordeal, and survived, only to be sucked into a second black hole, unfortunately this one killed him of course, because of the enormous amount of pressure exerted within the hole, he was crushed. That was a very long time ago, and since then my naturally trusting human nature has learned to become slightly more suspicious, and part of me wonders now if there may have been any foul play involved. I mean it's perfectly possible that somebody wanted the captain out of the way.

Well, I promised you the whole story, but if you're going to get the rest out of me, then you must believe in reincarnation and past life regressionists. The one that I saw and told me about a few of my many past lives, some 17,000 according to him, and that little story I just told you about the Centaur was part of one of my past lives. In fact, that was only one of my past lives, as that same Centaur, I was born again a second time as that same captain, but thousands of years later, about the time that the civilization known as Atlantis destroyed itself. It was then that we chose to help as many of them as we could to another continent by air lifting them. Also the same time I mentioned before when the star base was built next to the North Star as a base station during the rescue mission, (and is now used to monitor traffic going to, and coming form the planet Earth).

If you can't bring you're soul to believe in and accept the concept of reincarnation, then I see there isn't much point in telling you about a couple of other of my more interesting past life experiences, but for those of you that do happen to understand the entire concept, I think that you might get a kick out of these short tales.

In chronological order, unlike some of this novel, around the 12th century, at the time of the persecution of the Druids, I found myself, eventually captured by our enemies, the British I suppose, and along with the rest of my entire community, we were tortured and starved for six long years, as our captors kept us all crammed into great wooden heads, so crowded that we could only crouch for space, and fed only enough to keep us alive, and then finally they set the wooden heads on fire and burned us all alive…and why? They did it because we weren't the same as them, especially when it came to spiritual practices. Who knows what other insane reasons they must have come up with in order to justify their murders, which, incidentally, will catch up with them, as dharma does, if it already hasn't?

Well just so we can have a happier ending to this part of the story, I'll tell you about another life that I lived after those ones, that wasn't quite as fantastic, but still, the whole concept fascinates me, personally.

It was during the 16th century sometime, somewhere in the jungles of Borneo. I was a native of the land and lived with a tribe of others like me there. We weren't the kind of natives that were cannibalistic, although we did take the heads of our enemies in battle. Of course, we all lived happily ever after. Well at least until the end of that particular life anyway, I can't speak for the rest of the tribe, but personally that was one of the few actually peaceful lives that I can remember so far.

Before I get completely off track, I think I better continue with the adventures of Buzz Andrews. If you remember, he was just learning to fly a spaceship for the first time. It seems that he would not be wasting any time exercising his newfound freedom and talent. But, perhaps because of his great desire to engage in adventure, he would soon be finding himself in a situation that he would rather not be in, and his newly learned secrets would help him get there.

Now this was not his normal regular craft he took through the wormhole, or window, but it was more like a special capsule that had been designed specifically for the purpose of going through windows without being crushed. Although he was taught how to do this, he was also warned to be careful not to go there without supervision, or at least letting somebody know.

Of course, by this stage of his life, he had been accustomed to disregarding protocol of any sort. Before anyone could say boo, he was gone. Yeah, you guess it; he had let his curiosity get the better of him and gave in to the temptation to find out whatever awaited him on the other side. One would think that all the years of training he might have received while with the C.I.A. would have taught him to sniff out setups that are as obvious as this one appeared to be. Then again perhaps he did detect a frame, but went ahead and plunged headlong into the affair for whatever reasons may have encouraged him to investigate the future. Well this would probably be the second weirdest trip he would go on.

So anyway, he managed to propel himself through the wormhole via usage of the proper vehicle, and for a while found himself traveling at tremendously fast speeds, too fast to even estimate, for him anyway, all the way along he was observing different swirling colors and light in spirals and he seemed to be traveling though some sort of tunnel that was twisting and winding it's way to some unknown and fantastic destination. He tried with all his might not to be afraid in any way and remembered that any sign of fear could have a negative effect on the outcome of any given situation.

All of a sudden, he reached, or at least, seemed to be coming to the end of the tunnel, and for an instant, he had a thought about the stories he'd heard about people who had died and then come back to life only to tell stories of their adventures into the kingdom of light, and the 'tunnel' they all seemed to have traveled through, and he wondered if this was perhaps the same kind of tunnel, or at least something similar to the ones they spoke of. Suddenly he emerged out of the end of the tunnel and found himself plummeting down, very much affected by the pull of that old familiar gravity. And soon enough, he realized that he was indeed falling out of the sky, towards the planet down below as the atmosphere became lighter and lighter he could see finally, through the portals in his transport tube, that he was actually coming down directly out of a great blue sky, through the occasional cloud, downward towards a great blue ocean, or body of water, whether it was saltwater or not, he guessed, he would soon find out.

Find out he did. After initial splashdown, he managed to escape from the sinking metal tube that carried him safely through the wormhole, and tread water, keeping himself afloat. One little suck of the water instantly revealed that he would have a little less difficulty with his buoyancy, as the unmistakable taste of the seawater revealed its truly salty nature. Somehow the idea of being a little more buoyant because of the saltwater wasn't all that comforting. Not only did the saltwater keep him a little lighter and consequently nearer the surface, it also tended to have that effect on anything else that might be lurking in the dark and chilly waters. He began wondering just exactly what it was that he had done to deserve this. All of a sudden, he could see something floating along the surface of the water, but with all the up and down motion of the water, it was very difficult for him to be certain just what it was. Suddenly a huge dose of adrenalin rushed into his heart and circulated in his every vein, pumping him full of fear and several other uncalled for emotions...he was sure now, with his bad luck, that he was going to be swallowed up half alive and screaming for mercy only to be devoured by a huge man eating shark. Then again, who knows what planet he had discovered; maybe there weren't any sharks at all. Well he could only wait and see as the object got closer and closer to him.

By this time, the sun had begun to go down, rather quickly, he thought, and he noticed how tired he had become of treading water and trying to stay afloat. Not to mention, he was becoming very cold, and feared hypothermia would set in if he were not rescued soon enough.

Well, luck was with him this day, or so it seems. Sure enough he was about to be rescued by the floating object that he had spotted on the horizon. Indeed it appeared to be some kind of ship that was approaching him. However, just as he began to relax a little something from beneath the surface of water bumped into him and the adrenaline that had started to drain from his body began pumping back into his veins. He quickly submerged and found himself looking at not one, but several dangerous looking sharks curiously circling his position. He decided to return to the surface and check on that ship again. Sure enough it had pulled up close to him and lucky for Buzz, the people that were on board this ship were very much interested in rescuing him from the icy depths of the sea. So they did just that, by pulling up alongside of him, and helping him out of the water with a long rope ladder. Although he wasn't quite sure just how the strangers would treat him, he had to put his apprehension aside, for the moment anyway, and express his gratitude toward them for pulling him out of the water just in time and saving his life. In fact, he found it quite odd that they were making such a fuss over him, especially since he was a complete stranger to them...or so he thought. He would soon find out, however, that he wasn't the stranger that he thought he was and this of course would explain the 'royal' treatment that he was getting from them.

Well, it wasn't very long before they started to tell him a fantastic story about a savior, or a great hero that the entire planet was expecting to arrive in a flash of light out of the sky one day, and lead them all into a new and enlightened age, thereby bringing to an end the present state of tyranny and slavery that existed upon the land that they worked and lived on. It would seem, to them anyway, that Buzz Andrews was going to be this heroic person that they had all been waiting for, for so long. He was still experiencing a general state of shock from his journey, and from their fantastic story, when they arrived at the docks on the waterfront near the small coastal village where they lived. The sailors wasted no time at all in telling the townsfolk about the stranger they had rescued from the shark infested waters.

Now, some of you may be wondering, at this point, just what is the significance of all this? Well, there is some practical knowledge to be learned from this story, but more importantly, I'm including this short story in order that I may prepare you for things to come. In fact, it is Buzz's next major adventure that is really the most bizarre and unbelievable of all of his adventures, and if any of you were to doubt just one of his tales, the next one would be it, I'm quite sure. However, for those of you who may be inclined to believe all of this, I really must continue.

And so, Buzz finds himself being greeted by a huge landing party at the shore, as they begin to dock. Word travels fast in small communities. Before you could say, "boo" he found himself before a truly 'royal' family and their monarch. It was here that he learned the rest of the story about their hero savior that they were all awaiting the arrival of. He could see how they might mistake him for that long awaited fellow who would apparently come much the same way he had, but he really didn't think it was himself they were waiting for and prophesied about. In fact, the more they all began to treat him as that long awaited fellow, the surer he became that it just wasn't him.

Before he knew it, he had become the center of attention, and he had not only become the talk of the town but in their eyes, he was indeed the one they were waiting for. Soon enough, everyone was fussing over him, bringing him food and drink and gifts to honor him and perhaps to win him over some so that they might find favor in his eyes. Maybe this wasn't going to be so bad after all, he thought to himself. And he settled back to enjoy the attention they bestowed upon him. It wasn't long before he was full of food and drink when he realized how tired he had become from his little swim. The last thing that he could remember, he was trying to make sense of all the stories he had heard about the heroic one, and he wondered how he could possibly be that person. His last thought before his fatigue overcame him was that maybe, somehow, he really was the one they were waiting for all this time, and just maybe he could learn to like this now familiar story, and just maybe...he really was the one...zzzzzzz. That was it. He fell into a deep sleep. And as he slept, they carried him up a small hill to a private dwelling, with a single bedroom, laid him down on the bed, and left him to slumber and dream...all alone.

He dreamed vividly that night about Debbie, the beautiful, dark skinned woman that had saved him from the tiger, and in his dream they made love, again vividly, and he knew that he was in love with her.

Apart from that rather pleasant dream, the rest of the night was spent struggling through some less pleasant dreams, or semi sleepless images, mostly relating to the previous days' struggle in the water. Only in the semiconscious dream, Buzz spent most of the rest of the night fighting off sharks. In fact, he awoke more than once in a cold sweat, shaking off the monstrous vision of being devoured by sharks, or being pulled down under the water by them, gasping for oxygen. Finally he could rest no more and dragged himself out of bed, got dressed, and sat staring out over the water in anticipation of the coming sunrise. He could not help but think about the previous day's events and just how bizarre all of these days had been. Most of all, the crazy position he was now in, and how much he really didn't want to be a hero, or some sort of martyr, as these people were surely going to make him out to be if he stuck around. And that was it. Just then the morning sun started to creep up from over the water's horizon, as if to shine its very first light on the answer to his little dilemma. With that he knew what he must do. He must escape.

Before the last round edge of the sun had rolled itself over the horizon, Buzz had managed to get himself into one of the smaller sailboats that was left tied up and unguarded by the water's edge, and cast himself off into the shark infested waters, toward the distant, but visible mountains across the water. It wasn't long before he was out of sight and well on his way to his unknown but necessary destination. Although there was some apprehension on his part about sailing through this dangerous area alone, and only knowing the bare necessities of sailing, he was lucky to have shoved off on a fairly calm day. However, there seemed to be just the right amount of wind to enable him to come about again and again, until he had zigzagged his way to the opposite shore, which was only visible to him previously because of the mountains. Just before he reached the beach, he saw what he considered to be a sign from above. And he would soon find out that he wasn't wrong.

Directly up above him, in the clear blue sky, was some sort of light traveling across the sky. And just as suddenly as it appeared, it disappeared behind the mountain that was nearest his position where he was headed with his little boat upon the beach

Well now, wasn't that a curious thing that he observed?

Instantly he thought of his lost, but loved new friend and he hoped desperately that she had come to save him, or at least somebody from the Mother ship had come to rescue him. But then his hopes faded away as he watched the light go over the mountain, and it was gone.

Buzz was not the type to give up easily in the face of difficulty though, and he was determined to find out what this sign might be. Somehow he retained the feeling of hope, and that rescue was at hand. With that in mind he started up the beach toward the foothills and began his long upward climbing ascent toward the last seen position of the strange and guiding light. The climb, it seemed, was going to take him at least the better part of the day.

Around midday he stopped for one of his frequent looks back from whence he had come. In fact he had actually had the presence of mind to wrap up some of the leftovers from the previous day's feast. As he sat down to devour the last of it, he caught sight of one of the bigger sailing vessels of the people he had met coming toward the shore, as they could now plainly see his small craft beached there. He didn't panic, or even get scared much, as he knew they probably meant him no harm. Even so, he decided against sticking around to see just what they did have planned for him, if anything. He quickly finished his lunch, and resenting the fact that he wouldn't be able to linger and lounge in the lazy afternoon sunshine, he pulled himself up again and started back on his way up the mountain. To what he was sure would somehow be the answer to his prayers.

Every once in a while he turned and looked to see if the posse was still after him. Sure enough, they kept right on coming. But, at least they weren't gaining on him. This little chase went on for the rest of the afternoon. Now they all began to notice that it would very soon be getting dark, and as far as the posse was concerned, they would have to make a decision soon as to whether they would stay camped on the mountain overnight and continue the search in the morning, or just call it off completely and hope for the best. Perhaps their newfound messiah would return on his own accord. They decided that they should stay there on the mountain for the night, and make a decision as to whether or not they should continue the search for him in the morning.

The oncoming darkness of the night did not deter our hero from pressing onward toward his destination, as he felt even more strongly than before that he was soon going to find the answers to his prayers. Not to mention the fact that he was nearly at the crest of the mountain and that it seemed to level off some at this altitude, and the path he was walking on seemed to be leading him directly toward a passage between the peaks. Just what was on the other side of the passage was unknown to him as yet, but was somehow extremely appealing.

As he carried onward and still slightly upward by the light of the moon, he began feeling more and more like he was almost ready to arrive home. Different thoughts were going through his mind as to just why he was feeling that way. Would he be soon living there atop the mountains, as if he were some sort of sage or mountain man or something?

Well, if he were going to continue living at all, he would soon have to find himself something to eat. Surely there must be something around that could be considered safe for human consumption, and perhaps even nutritious. The people that he met on the previous day seemed to be healthy enough. They certainly were by no means 100% vegetarian either. However, it was also apparent that they weren't keeping much livestock around. So there would have to be plenty of creatures around that he could hunt and hopefully capture, and maybe even cook!

Just then he noticed that he was getting very close to the other side of the passageway. With a surge of excitement, and even a little adrenalin, he forgot completely about this hunger for a moment and he began to run along the pathway until he arrived at the end of the passage. From there he could see by the light of the moon that he was about to enter a huge and rather beautiful looking valley. Sensing he was on the verge of a great discovery, he crouched down to a squatting position (just in case there was a deer or something that he might be able to take by surprise). He didn't want to blow any possibility that he could soon be dining on some freshly caught wildlife.

His mouth began to water at the mere thought of it all when suddenly something caught his eye; something he could only describe as movement seemed to grab his attention. It was only for a second… and then there was only stillness. He held his breath as he watched for further signs of life. He was sitting very still and quiet when all of a sudden his stomach let out a bellowing, growling noise, as if to warn any nearby prey not to mess with him. He realized for the first time that there was just as much chance of him stumbling across; well let's say a tiger, or some other dangerous animal, as there was of coming to meet with something a little more bite sized. At this point, a little fear was injected into him, but not enough to overcome the nagging, relentless hunger howling in the pit of his stomach. Still, there was no further movement as he strained his vision across the valley, looking again and again, over and over, yet still nothing unusual for his senses to report. He might not have been quite so relaxed had he known what the people of that world had come to believe about this particular area that he was now crouching in, waiting for a sign, of anything.

But of course he had no way of knowing that they believed, religiously, that the entire valley that he was now entering was considered off limits to all the people there, and as well, they felt very strongly that the valley he was now seeking safety in was extremely haunted. And for this reason, not one of the superstitious people of that world would enter into the valley for fear that they would never return alive, or at all.

There is really no point in getting into too much detail about just what the people based their fear of this place upon. But once you discover the real activity that was going on around there, I think you'll have all the explanation you need to understand the basis of their superstition.

There was indeed a sort of spiritual haunting of this immediate area. You might call it more correctly, an occupation, rather than a haunting. The residents of this area, the spiritual ones, were not normally seen in a physical state. They had commonly been observed in their natural state; that of a light form, just like the glowing orb that Buzz had observed earlier that day when he was climbing the mountain and noticed what he thought was a sign from somewhere…hopefully from his previous hosts on the Mother ship.

Then again, maybe they weren't looking for him at all; perhaps they were happy to get rid of him, or possibly they even planned the whole thing. Who can say, maybe that was all just his paranoid delusions. He decided to continue to hope for the best, and as he stood to rise and stretch his legs, he gasped in a deep breath in wonder, amazement, and shock as his eyes beheld the sights that were now before him. (And he thought by now that nothing would be too surprising). But surprised he was, as he watched the whole valley before him become completely illuminated by the natural light and glowing of the same kind of light that he had seen earlier that day; only they were all changing color, and not one of them seemed to be the same color as another at any one time.

Staring in wonder and amazement, he rubbed his eyes and looked on in continued disbelief until he could take no more and he simply had to believe. He was trying to believe that these lights were somehow related to his friends back on the Mother ship.

Well, whether they knew it or not they were slightly related to each other, at least on a spiritual level. As Buzz would soon find out, the lights did not directly represent the interests of his friends, but they did represent their own interests and, as he would also soon find out, they were about to directly assume the responsibility of Buzz's great interest in returning himself to his friends.

At that precise moment, Buzz became highly emotional and found himself filled with an overwhelming homesickness and an overpowering desire to return to his friends and their present home base on their craft.

Without a further thought he got up and darted out from his

hiding spot and ran towards the area where the lights seemed to be gathering and swirling around in a circle, as if they were caught up in a tornado or a whirlwind reminding him of a cat or a dog chasing its own tail. He knew that he must try to contact these intriguing lights in the sky, although he had no idea just exactly how he would go about doing it. As he got closer and closer to them, they began to scatter every which way as they ascended away from the ground. By the time he reached the spot directly below where they were swirling around, they had all but disappeared from the immediate area, as if they were afraid of him. Frustrated, he just stood there waving his arms in the air as if to signal them to come back and meet with him. To his amazement, one of the lights broke away form the group and started to fly directly towards Buzz! The closer that it got to him, the brighter it got, until it was almost within reach.

At that point, it stopped right in front of him and began to change colors, going though the colors of the rainbow until if finally shone a brilliant golden hue lighting up Buzz himself and the ground and space around him, it grew in intensity and brightness until he could see a wispy figure begin to form from within the center of the glowing orb. He stood and watched in complete amazement as the smoky ethereal figure in the middle of the light became more and more defined. The clearer the image in the middle of the light became, the less and less the surrounding light appeared to shine, until there was absolutely no light left and in its place stood right there on the ground in front of Buzz a very real person, just like he was, alive and breathing! Needless to say, he was slightly surprised and a little taken aback, but this astounding event was only par for the course in his eyes, as he had seen more than just this one amazing occurrence in the past few days, so he was beginning to adjust himself to these surprises and his mind was becoming quite 'open' you might say, and even a little used to strange and sudden happenings such as this one.

So now he found himself standing there with his mouth wide open in wonder, facing what he hoped would soon be, if not already, a new friend and, quite frankly, not sure just what to say or how to begin. So he opened the conversation with a good old traditional introduction of himself, and hoped more than anything that this being in front of him could understand the language of English because that was the only language that Buzz knew. As it turned out, the stranger that stood before him knew more about Buzz than just the language he spoke. He not only knew how to communicate with Buzz, he also knew his name already, his deepest desire, which was to return to the Mother ship and be with his true love and soul mate Debbie, and of course he also knew that Buzz wanted to stay with her somewhere safe and he hoped that he would never again have to be so far away from her and feel so helpless to return. If this could not be so, Buzz could see no reason to go on living.

Buzz became almost overwhelmed with his feeling of intense desire to return, and found himself almost in tears in front of this empathetic being. He began to wonder if he had somehow managed to get himself into the presence of God. Before he could bring himself to ask who he was, the stranger spoke up and answered Buzz's question even before he could maneuver his thoughts from his mind to and through his mouth. The stranger wasted no time at all in explaining to Buzz that he was not God and went on to answer the rest of Buzz' questions almost before he could think them, let alone speak them. With some sense of relief, Buzz began to wonder if perhaps he had died already, maybe when he entered this world through the 'window' he had unwittingly met his death, even before the splashdown, and all that was happening to him was just a dream, for he often wondered if being dead was just like being permanently asleep and dreaming.

His new friend explained to him, again without being asked, that Buzz was indeed still very much alive and in his rightful body, even if he did seem to be completely out of place. He then went on to explain to him that all of this was meant as a learning experience for buzz, and as well, all the events of the past few days have had the intentions of a crash course in karma clearing. Which, according to the more violent events in his life, really needed to be dealt with before Buzz could continue on with the next course of things that were to happen to him in the very near future.

His new friend and spiritual guide went on to explain a little more about himself and where they were, how, and why, etc., in hopes of gaining enough faith from buzz, in him, so that he could help to save Buzz from this isolation and hopefully send him on his way back to the Mother ship, and his new friends there.

By now Buzz realized the two of them were having a very complete conversation with each other, entirely without the normal speaking of the mouth. In fact, the whole process of communication was now actually being accomplished only with the minimal effort of using their minds! This was rather new and exciting for buzz, and he supposed that he could quite easily get used to communicating in this way, telepathically, as it truly did require much less of an effort than speaking with the mouth. Buzz chuckled to himself as he thought perhaps that was the true meaning of the phrase 'speaking in tongues'.

So Buzz found out from his spiritual friend that the entities themselves, because of the very nature of being they were, as light forms, could obviously never be either just male or female, unless they transformed themselves into the human form, whichever would suit their present needs the most. They had reached this level of evolution only after many, many different lives and deaths in the physical plane of existence, so one could say that they had reached the state of being referred to as Nirvana. Which is the end of all physical forms of existence, except that they also seemed to have the ability to return to the physical state at will. Most of the time, however, was spent in the form that Buzz first witnessed them in; that is the spiritual state of being. Even so in this instance they opted to accept the responsibility of helping him to return to where he came from, that is, the Mother ship.

With that, his new savior began to walk across the valley of tall grass towards the other side, where there appeared out of the side of the rock face of the mountain side, what looked like the entrance to a cave. He motioned Buzz to follow him inside, and he explained to him that they had retrieved his original pod that he traveled here in from the bottom of the ocean earlier, which is probably why Buzz saw the light flying back over the water today. He went on to explain that if Buzz would trust them enough to climb back inside of the pod, that they were able to send him on his way back through the window from whence he came. Buzz was so overwhelmed with excitement that he actually hugged his friend and thanked him profusely before taking one last look of appreciation and, turning away to climb into the pod he said "thanks" one more time and hoped that they would meet again sometime, somewhere…and with that, the was off with one more great leap of faith.

In the account of his experiences, Buzz never really explained the exact method or propulsion that was employed in order to get him and his pod into space and back to the Mother ship, I'm assuming that this is because he was never told by his friends just how they had planned to do it. Whatever the method was though, it proved to be a very efficient and accurate means, as he flew in his pod right back to the exact place where he had departed from. No doubt the means by which his friends had moved him and the pod back through the window was some 'magical' method that, even if they had explained it to him he probably would not have understood, or perhaps he would have found it difficult to believe, which of course could have impaired all their efforts to transport him safely.

Wow! Talk about a smooth ride! He barely noticed any sort of pull or "g forces" at all. Before he knew it, he was right back where he had left the Mother ship, and he and his pod had successfully docked in the exact spot from where they had left! He simply could not find the words to describe his happiness at having been delivered back to his friends and true love. Buzz figured that the beings that he had just met were what you might call angels. And really, in every sense, that's just what they were. So with that, no further explanation of them was really needed. But he did tell his relieved friends the story of his disappearance, and, with great apologies, the story of his longing to return as well. Some of them began to wonder if he could really be trusted now after his disappearing act, but only the future could say just whether they would be proven right or wrong, and so they all agreed to give Buzz another chance, and they accepted his apologies and promises of never to take off like that again.

So he was allowed to continue on with his flight training, not to mention the wonderful times in between, when he was able to spend some absolutely magical nights alone with his loved one. In fact, 'magical' is almost an understatement describing the lovemaking abilities of his girlfriend, and the rest of the extraterrestrial women. (I would assume that the same goes for the E.T. men as well). Indeed they seem to possess a magical ability to sense the needs and desires of their partners in love, and during sex, in fact, once could say that they possess an uncanny ability to please their lover. I would guess this has something to do with the amount of time devoted to this event, and along with that, their empathic abilities are highly tuned, and have been perfected over the many years.

So Buzz had managed to gain the trust of his new companions again, but it would not be long before he would manage to breech their trust again. Although the next little incident would be a lot more provoked, though perhaps, the whole thing may have been avoided if Buzz could only have controlled his curiosity just a little bit more. Although, personally, I feel like in the end, maybe it's all for the better that he didn't.

CHAPTER 8

Buzz Gets a Second Chance;
Meets with NATO in Norway

And so without further delay, I feel that what I am about to tell you is probably one of the most incredible accounts of the events in the life of Mr. Andrews, and in fact, some of you may find this next story a little hard to swallow, although really it shouldn't be any more difficult to believe than what I've shared with you so far. But, all the same, I'd like to jog your memories just a bit, and ask you to look deep into your memory banks…back into the 70s. In fact I believe the year was 1976.

The place that the event occurred in was in the immediate area of Norway and its surrounding waters. The event was intended to be a gathering of the NATO forces. In fact, I can personally remember reading about the gathering of many battleships from some of the NATO involved countries in a local newspaper at the time; although they didn't say anything more than it was just a routine gathering of its forces. Who knows what may really have been going on there? Perhaps no more than they suggested, but by the time Buzz was finished with them, a whole lot more was going to happen, and here, for the first time, many of you can discover some of what really was going on.

Now although all of us, or at least those of us who read newspapers here on Earth, have the advantage of doing just that in order to keep relatively abreast of things going on. This was one luxury that Buzz, as an extraterrestrial, didn't have…or at least, that is to say, he didn't wake up with the news on his doorstep, as we might. So that when he came upon this huge gathering of warships parked in the waters off the Norwegian coastline, well, who can blame him for becoming slightly curious as such an ominous sight? At any rate, that's how this whole story begins, and perhaps spurred on by the memory of his last encounter with warships on the water, buzz decides that this view of things he has come across is far too interesting to merely pass over. I mean especially since now he has quite a bit more control over his craft, and therefore the resulting destiny of both he and his craft.

Quite frankly, it seems that this little taste of control and power would be far too delicious to even consider trying to control. With one last shocking glance at the vision down below him, he dove his craft downwards, directly towards Norway and what seemed to be the central base for commands there. In fact, he did a wonderful job of landing directly in the centre of things there, much to the surprise of everyone, especially the General in Command. It seems that he managed to land his craft right smack dead in the centre of what looked like a landing pad of the base, because of the big X in a circle that was plainly visible to any pilot. He was now parked directly on top of it! Of course several armed soldiers instantly greeted him, as his arrival was completely unexpected, and I suppose they may have felt a little threatened by this unannounced arrival. Well then, this seems like a good time to introduce myself, he concluded, and within a couple of seconds Buzz had tapped into their computer with his ships' computer. Before they could say, "boo" his image was being projected onto the screen in their control room, and he could see the General that was in the control room on his monitor.

Now the General didn't seem to take too kindly to this interruption and began to make all sorts of demands upon Buzz, such as who he was, where he came from, what was his purpose for being there completely uninvited, etc. The General became even more frustrated when Buzz refused to come down out of his craft and surrender himself to them. So he began to threaten him with all kinds of nasty actions. Of course none of their threats could even begin to frighten brave Mr. Andrews, as he was feeling particularly invincible in his new toy. He seriously doubted that they could penetrate his shields or harm him in any way, and upon his statement of these feelings, the General became even more frustrated and seemed to be losing his patience. I mean, Buzz did try his best to explain who he was, but this wasn't god enough for the General. He wanted Buzz out of his craft and on his knees. Well by this time, Buzz was also losing his patience and decided that the man he was speaking to in the control room was being rather rude and demanding, and Buzz decided that he couldn't really trust the man. A wise decision no doubt and he would do well to remember this, as he would soon find out.

The General didn't seem to be buying any of Buzz's explanations at all and was sure that he could convince Buzz to 'cooperate' with them, so he began to make some serious threats to take action against Buzz. Buzz merely sat there and said, "Go ahead see if I'm joking with you. Do what you want to my craft. You won't be able to hurt me or penetrate my defensive shields."

That was all the General needed to hear to provoke him into action. I think what really did it was when Buzz basically stated a few facts about where he had come from and the kind of weaponry they had available to them, the number of warriors on his side, and their basic superiority. He may also have said something like it was futile for the people of Earth to resist their forces, and that they all needed to learn to live together in a more harmonious fashion, and generally just be a more peaceful people, etc. Of course Buzz took it upon himself to do all of this without asking anyone that may have been superior to him, or getting any kind of sanction from his buddies at all. Yes, you could say that his diplomatic method seemed a bit primitive; however, Buzz felt that he was only doing the right thing for the best interests of all parties concerned. I'm quite sure that he was enjoying this little display of 'diplomacy' of his, although I suspect he may have begun to become frustrated with the General's manner, and he was about to find out that the General's diplomatic manner left a lot to be desired.

So by now the General had threatened to napalm bomb Buzz and his craft if he didn't surrender immediately! Well, Buzz had no intention of doing that so he told them to go right ahead. They did. Within a few seconds, a screaming fighter jet flew directly over Buzz and delivered the fiery bomb directly up Buzz and his craft.

Fortunately it had absolutely not effect on either him or his scout ship. He wasn't surprised, but they were, and he was happy, and they weren't. So they continued their attack upon his craft with whatever they had handy, bullets, hand grenades, etc., but to no avail. They soon realized that it was going to take more than what they felt was safe for them to try right there on the base...and they were in no way interested in being intimidated by the rhetoric of Mr. Andrews. He seemed to be demanding of them, and slightly ahead of their time, to say the least. Yet here he was, still staring, rather presumptuously, I might add, directly back at the General from inside his monitor screen. So they talked a bit more with each other and this little standoff grew into a full fledged test of strength and show of power. During the course of their conversation, one thing led to another and Buzz ends up bragging about the abilities of his scout ship and the futility of their even trying to do anything to him. Well, it seems that they were easily goaded into a little demonstration of his ability to defend himself. So Buzz agreed to let them try to shoot his craft out of the sky and he would not retaliate in any way. Well, let me be a little more specific. He agreed to let them test the effectiveness of their weapons against the strength of his shields. That is really what the demonstration was supposed to be all about. However, as it happened, Buzz discovered that he couldn't really trust his new acquaintances.

So as they were all flying to a predetermined area, out over the water, with Buzz flying a little bit ahead of a small group of a few fighter jets, they suddenly broke their flying V formation down the middle, and from out of the centre and directly behind comes this flying black triangle shaped object at a very high rate of speed, and within a couple split seconds it opened fire on buzz and his craft without any warning! This was not only unexpected, but a breech of their verbal agreement, which was to test any of the firepower, or weapons that were available to the conventional fighter jets that they had.

Well, since they had caught him off guard in this way and by opening fire on him before they all had reached the intended spot, he actually thought that this could really be the end of it all for him, and even reminded him of the bazooka flash that he had once faced. Buzz didn't even have his shields up yet as they were still heading to the test area. Fortunately for Mr. Andrews, his scout ship was capable of raising its own shield in case of any unseen surprise attack, such as this was, and so, it did just that and not a moment too soon either. Just a split second after the ship raised its own shields, the full force of the blast from the other, ominous and evil looking black craft, struck the force field around Buzz's craft with such power that the shock of it rocked and shook his vehicle!

It then screamed past him and fled away very fast. By this time he realized what was going on and gathered his senses and began to pursue the black triangle at such a high rate of speed that they left the fighter jets behind them and out of range and distance of eyesight. He followed the craft down the east coast of the United States, and then west. Being his first real taste of serous battle with his new craft, he was unable to keep right on the tail of the 'bad guy', and he lost him somewhere near California's west coast. Buzz felt sure that he hadn't permanently lost his enemy, but that it had merely descended somewhere in the immediate vicinity, and that it would sooner or later ascend again, and Buzz planned to be right there ready and waiting for him when he did.

So he parked his craft up above the area where he felt it had gone down and sat back and relaxed a bit, watching the skies and the ships monitor, waiting for the return of the ship that had attacked him.

Well it soon became clear that he might be waiting there for a while, as the enemy did not seem to be coming up in any great hurry. Buzz decided to use the time to get better acquainted with his craft and he spent close to a week practicing maneuvers and hovering up there in the clouds waiting for the guy to return. During that time, he found plenty of things to do; although I'm sure he was quite cramped and would have rather been somewhere else. He even spent a great deal of his spare time watching local television stations on his ships' monitor, as he was able to tune into virtually any kind of communications signals from earth.

Buzz was rewarded for his patience and intuition. After about a week of hiding in the clouds, he spotted the little black triangle on his monitor ascending in the exact area he suspected it might. It came out of hiding and set off through the skies in a southerly direction, seemingly unaware that it was being followed every step of the way by Mr. Andrews in his little scout ship. They had not gone very far south at all when the black ship turned and headed eastward towards Bermuda. All the while Buzz managed to keep a safe enough distance from the other craft so that he would not be detected, and I really must say that I think he did a wonderful job of tailing the other guy right from the beginning.

We really must wonder what he had in mind, or what he was thinking he might do when he caught up with the fellow that attacked him one week earlier. At any rate, he decided to try and tail him further and see where he was headed, so he remained out of sight and kept a safe enough distance from him so that he would not be detected, but close enough so that he wouldn't lose him, and it seemed to be working just fine. The black ship led Buzz directly to a 'window' that is located within the Bermuda Triangle. Then he observed the black ship going through the window and seemingly disappearing. He waited a few seconds and then entered into the window himself, which he could not have done with any conventional typed of aircraft that is available here on Earth today, they just are not constructed of strong enough material to get through unassisted without being crushed. Fortunately, he wasn't in any conventional type of craft and he was able to follow the 'bad guy' through the window. Upon reaching the other side, there was just enough time for him to witness the black ship flying into some sort of portal within the earth's crust itself, and this made Buzz even more curious as to where this guy might be headed.

All around him, everywhere he looked, all that he could see was gleaming white snow and ice. Assuming that they were still on Earth, Buzz figured that they must be somewhere near the South Pole. He decided to follow that black craft into the portal, or opening in the ice and snow, and find out where he was going...presumably some sort of underground secret hideaway. Now Buzz had seen a lot of far out stuff in the last few weeks, but he still had room in his senses to be a little surprised when he set eyes upon the sights that were before him now as he wound his way through a long narrow passage and emerged from the other end.

When he came to the end of the long tunnel, it opened out into a vast cavern within the earth and all along both sides of the cavern walls he could see that somebody had built into the very sidewall of the rocky cavern, windows and doorways, etc. as if many people were living within the cavern walls. The whole entire place was huge, and as he flew from one end to the other, keeping a close eye on the exit hole where he had entered from, he came to the realization that he had stumbled across a place that he had been told about earlier. Or at least, from what he had seen to far, he was sure that this must be the place they told him about, where Satan and his closest buddies were hiding out and living. It was a place that was some 200 kilometers below the surface of the planet Earth.

Which means that they were somewhere directly beneath the surface of the part of the Earth's crust that we call the South Pole. That explains all the ice and snow that he saw just before entering into the tunnel. Wow! Awesome! Buzz thought to himself, or perhaps he said it out loud. No matter, this was a once in a lifetime opportunity indeed, and one that he would probably never get again. Not in a whole entire lifetime could he ever even hope to gain such a discrete entrance to this place. If he were to go without leaving his mark, he might never get another chance like this. He had to take advantage of the situation while he was here, and he didn't have to think for very long in order to decide just what he was going to do to have them remember him.

In fact, no sooner had he come to the end of the long cavern and its neat rows of cave fronts, than he had noticed the black ship that he had been following earlier, and without a second thought, he fired on it directly and destroyed it with one laser blast. He flew through the debris and did a U-turn and bolted back from whence he had come, blasting the walls of the cavern and their doors and windows that were cut into them so perfectly, as he flew towards the place he got in. As he made his escape, he blasted as many times as he could against the cavern walls, causing enormous explosions as he went and a great amount of damage. It was quite clear to him that they had not anticipated an attack on themselves of any sort, at least that's how it appeared to Buzz. This all seemed to be too easy. Maybe he was a little hasty in his thinking, for just as he completed that last thought, out of somewhere he managed to pick up a tail of two or three black triangular ships just like the other one, and they were seriously angry with him for attempting to destroy their little secret hideaway, and for the damage he'd already done.

However this time he was more prepared for them, and as he already had his shields up, that left him a few extra seconds to fire back upon them. Instantly he managed to destroy two of the three that were in pursuit, and he kept on firing at the walls of the cavern causing a lot of damage as he went. Some of the debris and smoke from the laser blasts from his craft were also helping to obscure him from the sights of the craft that still was in pursuit, making it even more difficult for the bad guy to take aim. Buzz was not particularly concerned with the one that was following him anyway, because so far, his shields had proven to be stronger than theirs, so he continued firing upon the cavern walls in order to cause as much damage as he possibly could before he left their little hideout. He was quite sure that this would be the last time that he was going to be able to do something like this, here, so he wanted to leave a serious impression upon his enemies. It was like his own specially delivered message to them, sort of a reply to all of their previous attacks upon him. I suspect that he was not only really enjoying this adventure, but that he felt this was his duty, that is to say, he was getting even, for all their dark deeds from the past. This also enabled him to release a lot of anger that they had caused him to carry.

Well by now he was coming to the other end of the cavern, and he could see the entrance/exit hole from whence he'd come. This brought a big smile to his face and an ear piercing shout of delight and excitement, into, and out of his throat.

It was beginning to look as though he was going to get out of there with his life, or at least there seemed to be a very good chance of that now that he had the opening to the cavern in his sights. However, he still had that one ship following him, and, no doubt there would soon be a few more in pursuit of him as soon as they had enough time to assemble a posse. Buzz took in a deep breath, and with that he swooped in to the long, narrow tunnel that would lead him to the surface of the planet and finally, the wide open spaces. He wasn't there yet though, and he was so busy navigating his way through the tunnel that he had a difficult time returning any fire to the vessel that was in pursuit of him.

For a while there he even tried to cause a cave in behind him, but the task proved to be just a little too tricky for him under the present circumstances. What with the black triangle that was firing upon him constantly, and the high rate of speed that was involved, there wasn't much time to think about anything else other than outrunning the fellow. Remember, that basically all of the command functions of the type of craft that Buzz was in are performed simply by thinking! The pilot has a helmet upon his head and his thoughts, or the transmission of his idea is picked up by the helmet and transmitted to the spacecraft's computer intelligence, and the command is carried out all in a split second. So therefore, we say that the ship is thought operated. And at that particular moment, Buzz had a lot on his mind, it was all he could do to fly himself safely and quickly through the tunnel and keep himself ahead of what seemed to be a more experienced flyer. Never mind the fact that the guy happened to be shooting at him constantly. But his shields held up, and quite often the other guy would land the full force of his blast on the cavern wall. This too was having its effect of the surrounding structure.

Who knows how much more of this blasting the walls could stand up to? He was half hoping that the tunnel would collapse at any moment, but there was always the danger of getting caught in the cave in.

Finally he began to see the light at the end of the tunnel. And before he knew it, he found himself and his craft emerging from the long cavern, and out over the frozen and barren tundra. Now he could concentrate on getting rid of his pursuer, once and for all. Fortunately, previously when he went through the window of the Bermuda Triangle, he made a point of recording the exact longitude and latitude, and altitude of the window, so that he would be able to find his way back through it. He managed to locate and pass through the window just a few seconds ahead of the black triangle that was in pursuit of him. Immediately after Buzz went through it, he flew his craft into a position, just above the exit point from the window, and parked his craft up there behind a cloud. Once the ship's sensors detected the other craft coming through, he dropped out of the cloud cover, and fired directly upon the only craft that seemed to be the entire posse at the moment. Bingo! Again, he managed to take out the enemy with one single blast from his laser weapon! It was a great relief for him that these black triangular ships appeared to be no match whatsoever for the superior technology of the Federation vehicle that he was now piloting.

He waited there for a little while longer to see if any more of them would be coming after that last one to try and catch him. But, as it appeared, they seemed to have given up the chase; perhaps they weren't willing to risk an all out attack on the Inter Galactic Federation of the Free Worlds. Which reminded him he would soon have to be reporting back to the IFFW, and he wasn't really looking forward to that.

Still, after a few minutes up there in hiding behind the cloud, he decided that he had better get back home and face them all with his story. After all, it had been at least a week since he left the Mother ship, and he sorely missed his beloved Debbie. Well that's okay, he would soon be able to spend all the time in the world with her, as he found himself grounded for awhile as a direct result o the adventures and misadventures of the past week or so.

The IFFW had decided that he was just too much of a risk right now, there were a lot of things going on at that time with the Federation, and there still is for that matter, and let's just say that they did not want to jeopardize any of the plans they had for the Imperial army.

So Buzz and Debbie were allowed to move on down to the good old planet Earth together and live happily ever after for a while, or at least, well who can really say how long they'll be here before they head off into the wide open spaces together again? Hopefully, things will be much more peaceful for them next time they decide to fly, but somehow, I have a feeling that things will probably get crazier between the IFFW and the Imperials before they become more sane.

CHAPTER 9

Intergalactic Peace Treaty of 1908: One Million Dollar Landing Pad

Now if I could just try to jog your memories a little bit again, although most of you probably won't recall this little newspaper item I'm about to tell you about, some of you may. As I said earlier, all this was happening one season in 1976… there was an earthquake reported, or rather a series of them in the area of the South Pole, right near where Buzz discovered the secret hideaway of Satan and his associates. However, the real reason for the tremors wasn't revealed to the public at all. It was written up, but not explained accurately until now. No doubt not many journalists could access that kind of information through any of Satan's channels in the government. Now you know how an all out war might affect our planet. Just a small-scale battle like the one Buzz was involved in with the black triangles was enough to cause tremors and earthquakes within the Earth.

Well, with all of this information I've related to you so far, one can certainly and justifiably wonder just what will become of all of us who have become so accustomed to living here on the good old planet Earth, especially if we consider that solar giant I told you about, 180 years is not very far away. Especially when you consider the possibility of living longer than the usual human being on Earth does presently. If you choose to believe that there just might be an elixir of eternal life, and that one day you may have the option of prolonging your life to 1,000 years, and further with cloning and soul transmigration! Then, suddenly 180 years doesn't seem so far off, does it?

It may offer you some amount of comfort to think that the Intergalactic Peace Treaty of 1908 might actually do some good. This was an obvious effort on the part of the IFFW and the Imperials to approach some sort of peaceful existence with each other, but in view of all that I've learned about either of these factions, their relationship seems to be headed for more troubled time than not, and war seems inevitable, however unpleasant and difficult it may be to believe, it may also be necessary nonetheless.

It may also be of some comfort to some of you who might believe, that Rael was instructed by the Council of Eternals, leaders of the Elohim, that he should, upon returning to Earth, find a friendly land and build a landing pad in anticipation of the arrival of them, sometime in the very near future. I believe that he was told to approach the government of Israel first, but that if they refused to give him permission to build it in their country, that he should go to a more neutral country like Switzerland or somewhere similar, and to tour the world and petition the ordinary people of Earth for the funds to finance the building of the pad. They, the Elohim, even gave Rael exact measurements of the dimensions and layout of the entire landing pad, saying that it should be built exactly according to their specifications. Now that it has been almost forty years since Rael first met the Elohim, I wonder if he has completed his mission or if he is still trying to raise the money for the project? I remember when Rael came through our town a few years ago, somebody that I knew happened to cross paths with him, describing him to a 'T' physically, including the medallion that he wears, and saying that he rode upon a large 'hog' (a Harley Davidson motorcycle), I was glad to hear that his mission was well underway. I knew that when they brought him back to Earth they landed in France.

I would hope that all of you would find it as shocking as I did, when I discovered that the President of the council of Eternals does not believe in the eternal soul. However, I suppose that it should have been obvious if you think about the way they use their knowledge of DNA and cloning. They believe that by burning the physical body in their huge pyre like machines, and never cloning that body, that the soul is somehow trapped or locked up as if the spirit belonged to that body only! So "Hell" merely becomes a crematorium, nothing more, and "Heaven" is simply the planet that the Elohim live on, one light year from Earth. Now you tell me…what real concrete proof do any of us really have that says Heaven and Hell exist? All that we really have to go on is our faith in a few religious books. Now tell me, how many books have been written about UFOs? How many of you have seen for yourselves, and know for a fact that ETs exist? A lot more I bet, that the amount of you who have been to 'Heaven' and can talk about it. However, if we include near death experiences, I suppose that a fair number of us have had, at least a glimpse through the doorways that lead to both of those places. As long as I'm summarizing here, I guess that I shouldn't forget that Satan doesn't appear to be all that scary either. It's nice to be able to keep things in perspective, they have a tendency to get out of hand and perspective if we don't take a long serious look at the way it really is.

The longer and more seriously that I look at Yama Raja, the name that I prefer for our heavenly Father, as opposed to Jehovah (or God, which is far too vague for one person, as it really applies better to all of the creators), the more I am convinced that is his true identity and I feel that somebody should tell him of his striking resemblance to himself, as he is defined in the Bhagavad Gita, as the demigod who punishes the sinful after death, and rewards the faithful and the loving. Yes it seems that Jehovah has a double identity, or at least a secret one besides the one, which he already has. And the responsibilities that come with that identity are really not so very far from what he is already doing and planning to do. In fact, they seem to be identical. I would love to talk to him and see if he has ever noticed these similarities before as I have. Okay, I'll admit it, I also want to talk to him about his faith in the Great Spirit, or the "Holy Ghost" if you prefer. You know whom I mean. KRSNA!

My main concern is that he recognizes the truth about the eternal soul, not only for the benefit of atman, but also for the benefit of the general state of the universe. As it is, as long as he goes on thinking that there is no such thing as the soul, there is a definite danger the more evil ones, such as, let's say, Adolph Hitler, may have an easier time reincarnating back amongst the living and the physical existence, and risks such as that are totally unnecessary, dangerous, and completely unacceptable. As long as YamaRaja retains that old attitude and consciousness, I must say he'll be failing in his duties and letting his work pile up.

Since I've been writing this novel, I've heard a lot from my closest colleagues about how important it is for me to be able to prove what I say, or a least verify the sources of my information, so as to lend as much credibility to the facts as possible. Well, I hope that they can understand that I do realize the importance of all that, but that in some cases, even though I have the information relating to the source and can identify same, that I simply cannot and will not divulge that particular information if I feel that by doing so might in any way cause or bring trouble to those particular individuals. It is important, very important for me to protect my sources, and at the risk of sounding like a spinner of tall tales, or being labeled a 'liar' I really must stick to the writer's code of silence, for all parties concerned. It is unfortunate, but I'm sure that they, and y'all will understand why, and I can only hope that the true seekers amongst us will forgive my shortcomings on this matter, and let their faith, good sense, and inner self guide them so that they may judge for themselves if I am really out to deceive anybody, or truthfully, that I am only doing all of this so that anyone who really cares and wants to know more about the elusive creators may gain some insight, as I feel that they have the right to know and the faithful have waited long enough now for this knowledge.

I can't help but be reminded of similar cases where, for some ridiculous reason, the real truth about something is kept out of the mind of common knowledge, and because of that, many thousands of people are made to suffer! Specifically, I am referring to a very common and deadly disease called cancer. The source of the proof of this knowledge I am about to say is very common knowledge amongst the 'organic' health food community. There is a very simple and effective cure for that dreaded cancer, in fact, there are 3 or 4 specific items that can be taken in order to arrest cancerous growths and prevent them from even coming. At least one of them in particular has been tested and found to be extremely efficient in curing even lethal doses of cancer and radiation poisoning. I myself would prescribe all of these remedies for anyone with such an illness, if they were willing, as it is, what have they got to lose by trying it?

CHAPTER 10

Wheatgrass and Golden Seal

This miracle cure that I speak of is the juice of the young wheat plant... called wheat grass. Simply by sucking the juice out of the grass, from common and preferably organic wheat berries, while the young grass is still green, one can obtain not only a new lease of on life, but a renewed hope and healthy body as well. Further I will say to you skeptics out there, that it is not up to me to prove that what I've claimed is true, but I leave it up to you to disprove, if you can, which I sincerely doubt. The problem is, as it has happened before, when the government finds out about such miracle cures, they have a nasty tendency to try and silence anybody with such knowledge and keep the truth from getting out, thereby assuring themselves a position in 'research' and treatment of the diseases in their own way. As shocking and unbelievable as it is, it would seem that they would rather have everyone suffering and continuously paying for treatments that barely work, if at all.

I know this to be true, and a good example of this sort of behavior came up recently when they discovered that we in the health food community have been effectively using an herb called Goldenseal for some time now as an anti-mucal agent, and also as a topical and oral disinfectant. The government has recently made it almost impossible for us to market and sell this herb. It has all but disappeared from the shelves of the health food stores, and it is very difficult to find now here in B.C., Canada. I remember a few years ago, when they also wanted to gain access to our organically grown fruits and vegetables in order to irradiate them. We had to petition them religiously in order to prevent it from happening. They wanted to start with the potatoes and onions, but I'm sure if we had let them get even that far, that they soon would have gotten to the rest of it. I don't know if you have ever eaten anything that has been certified organically grown or not, but as I discovered when I was 15 years old, clean food is much sweeter and generally far better tasting and tender than food that is not organically grown. In this province, in order to obtain organic certification, a farmer must not use any kind of pesticides, keeping the soil free and clean from all such poisonous fertilizers and such for 3 years. Of course, further, the food must not be preserved in any way, including irradiation, and of course no other additives are allowed that are not clean and natural. The result is a product much like our ancestors used to eat, produced only with sun and rain and dirt. I could go on and on about how exciting and revitalizing a healthy diet can be, resulting in much more energy and a naturally 'high' feeling, but I think it is much better for you to find out for yourself. I should say that the more people that take an interest in their health and the health food community in general and the sooner they do it the better because there is a disconcerting rumor going around that the governments of Earth would like to make all natural herbs available to us only through prescription. This is something that must be stopped and can be fought successfully through petitions.

Unfortunately, I've discovered that most people will not go out and try something for the first time unless they have been 'turned on' to it already by a friend or some other trustworthy person. That is such a shame. I guess I can understand though, that they don't really know what they should be looking for, in the way of organically grown food. However, anything that one can get anywhere else, for the most part, is also available at the local health food store. With a few exceptions all they really need do is find all their favorites, in organic form.

One common fallacy that I would like to shed some light on is the misconception that one cannot find enough protein in a health food store… this is not true. There is just as much, if not more protein available in the health food store, and the protein that there is much more easily assimilated and utilized by the body! Besides that, the body's first source of energy is derived from carbohydrates.

Well, I've said a lot about curing cancer and irradiation poisoning, but what I've neglected to tell you about is one of the common, and yet unrecognized sources of these two deadly illnesses. For obvious reasons, the people who irradiate your food do not tell you that the irradiation can be a source and cause for both of those diseases. Perhaps they just don't know it yet. Well I'm here to tell that what Monique Khuse told me; that the present way, in which the people of the earth do split the atom, leaving out one element that is necessary for balance, does weaken and destroy the flesh. Without the enlightened writings of this wonderful woman, Monique, I'm not so sure that I would have ever made the connection between food irradiation and skin cancer. I can tell you from experience though, that I myself have amazed and astounded not one, but two professional medical doctors. When a friend of mine came to me complaining of open red sore areas that had mysteriously appeared upon the surface of his skin, I immediately applied a mixture of aloe-vera plant juice, or perhaps it was vitamin E oil. Either way, I mixed the gooey substance with goldenseal powder in order to get the powder stuck to the skin where the sore was. Within a few short days my friend returned to the doctor's office where he had previously been to see if they could help him to cure the sores, but they could do nothing but grow frustrated at the futility of their efforts to cure him. The physician just could not believe that the sores were completely healed and almost gone, and with great surprise and curiosity, asked him how he had managed to get rid of the sores, when he could not.

A short time later, another friend of mine came to me with the same problem and again, within two or three days, I had managed to clear up the sores completely using the goldenseal mixture. And again, his doctor was left in bewildered confusion trying to figure out how I had done it.

It is at this point in our journey that I would like to share with you, after great deliberation, another interesting item that has magically 'fallen' into my hands, thanks again to the most pleasantly surprising and wonderful woman…Monique Khuse.

Yeah, that's right, I said after great deliberation. Meaning, I just couldn't decide whether or not to display this sort of information for y'all to see. Mostly, I guess my indecision stems from knowing that even if I were to share this with you, it probably won't do anything to really further the space flight travel program. However, the deciding factor for me was that there had been rumors of captured extraterrestrial crafts that nobody can figure out how to fly. Well, I've decided that the instructions that I've managed to get hold of just might match up with one of the UFOs. However, all I can do to further this situation is to provide these flight instructions, the rest is up to the owners of the captured crafts.

I must say, however, that I do not recommend anyone actually try to fly a strange craft like that without the real and true owners and creators of the craft present to oversee the flight, or at least, they should have some kind of voice contact with the inventors of the craft. Who knows…if somebody actually succeeds in starting the engines of the craft, they might be able to obtain actual voice contact with the home basestation of the craft, as the ignition sequence does include steps that require a clearance procedure and a statement of the intended destination of the pilot and craft, before they can take off and fly.

Instructional Symbols

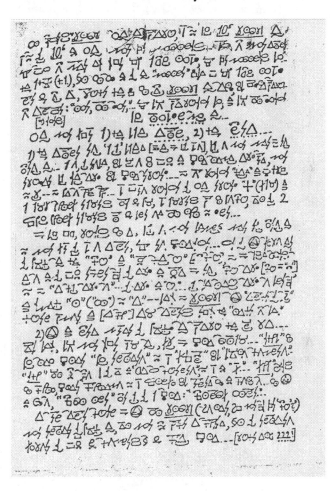

This to mean the instruction after liftoff from this condition to

ant system. There open up the right understanding computer system. There instructing the personnel of the travel condition ahead.

This to be the instruction to open the main operating switch. To be found on this computer of this one ship. All ship not to be equal in their construction. This one can be read. Then to be on the right vibration of sound. To form through electronic equipment of any sound equipment of this physical level. There to open all system. There to be waiting to the next response from the commander. The sound to be of high pitch sound vibration. There turning on all communication system through the ship and other command of home base. There to collect in the edge of this system of earth condition. To be out 1000 feet of unseen vibration.

This to be the opening of still other computers needed for the connection to all machinery of this ship. There with the right mind understand to open all.

This to mean of connection needed between home base. There entering data needed for the mission ahead. Opening this system to be of 4 computers on this one ship. There home base to be the same value. There to contact the right symbol to the right vibration to be of mind of electronic equipment. Carried in the hand of those voyagers. This to be the right vibration to follow in sequence to the symbol. There to be music sound vibration. There to formulated to this day being to understanding the password of entering this system.

This to mean enter all connection to the main powerhouse with the right symbol to the next explanation.

This to mean both connections at the time the symbol to be found on this one computer. There needed those two electronic devices activated at the same time.

Those instructions to be there for the personnel. Giving them the understanding of the working of this power plant. Main energy supply to all system. There to matching exactly with the control mechanism of this one ship. Those to be corresponding to exact degree before the departure of this one. There to be check for all working condition. Those symbol understood by those being of their meaning. Those condition not to be understood yet by those being. This one symbol only there for the personnel instruction to be all in order of thing. This one not to be there again. Other computer to turn on to this program. To register such not to let this vehicle depart to any condition. Those symbols must be all operated with the mind or device of those personnel. Those to have also connection to the construction of the ship. Understanding its working knowledge symbolic message.

This to mean the knowledge needed to open all communication system between other computer. There to be working all for the command of this personnel. Those symbol over in the right order to give home base all instruction of this mission ahead. There also recording all data needed for further study of this. There given all knowledge. All to be included in this system once open. There to include the main powerhouse to its working condition and maintenance. This one to remain in perfect order of things.

This to mean all system in order for the lifting off system of this one ship.

You can see from the illustrations above that only a small portion of the entire page is actually translated and explained. You may also notice the similarity of the appearance of the foreign language to some of the ancient Egyptian texts. It would appear that the two strange writing styles do show some semblance towards one another. You may also have noticed some fragmentation in the sentences and other grammatical errors. I left them that way intentionally because that is the way that I received them and I thought that it was kind of cute the way that the E.T.'s spoke in our language, somehow it seems to lend credibility to the source.

I can't tell you what the rest of the writing on that page means, but the few phrases that are explained may help someone to program a UFO to take itself back from where it came, and send a message of 'good will' and intentions home with it, in case it somehow manages to return itself to its birthplace. And of course any cargo or passenger that has enough 'guts' to go with it, may also reach that unknown destination. Imagine the excitement of returning to its place of origination with it, and the moment of anticipation as you stepped off of the craft upon arrival to meet its makers! Sounds like a very interesting and stimulating adventure. How many of you would actually volunteer for such a mission if it were at all feasible? And further, how many of you would only do it for money?

One thing I can tell you though, is that in order to operate the craft, one has to program its computers with the use of a hand held device much like the ones that we use here on Earth when programming a television or stereo…you know, a remote control unit? Without that, I seriously doubt that these instructional steps will be of any practical value to anyone except to tease their imagination and curiosity. Let's hope that this remote control hand unit is still intact and can be located within the craft itself.

If we can manage to get that far, I might as well tell you now, that by holding the remote in hand and thinking of the images and clearly imagining the proper sequence as indicated on the instructions, one must then somehow transfer the thought of the images, through the remote, which may also require some sort of helmet or headset to communicate with and help to transfer the image of the pilot's thoughts about the proper sequence of the ignition and preflight, and flight instructions, including the request for flight clearance from the base station.

We can only assume they are friendly or they would not have let all this stuff fall into our hands. Maybe they are trying to test us and see just how we react to their unusual inventions. Who knows, and will we ever find out? I for one do hope that we do.

By now I've told you a lot about some of the different kinds of flying crafts in use by some of the different groups of extraterrestrial beings. However, I've neglected to tell you about one of the features in particular that I think will not only astound you, but will probably sound so farfetched that at least some of you won't even believe it. I've only recently found out about this particular amazing function through that same wonderful connection of mine, who I happen to trust and believe in. I also have no reason to doubt him when he tells me that he's been up several times (in a flying craft); he just has too many interesting items of evidence to show that he speaks from very valuable experience. I would be a fool to doubt him after all that I have seen.

I've also seen a number of very interesting videos on the subject of ETs and their crafts, but the one that has caught my eye the most lately, besides the beautiful picture of Samjese (pronounced *sam-yassee*) that is, is the video of the two different types of Pleiadian ships that are the most commonly sighted from Earth. They both look very similar to each other except for a few slight differences in design that are visible. And one very important and distinct difference in their design that allows the newer, improved craft and its passengers to travel through time!

Now isn't that something? We've all seen the concept in movies, or read such stories, or thought about it or whatever, but I'm now here to tell you that it's not all-just fantasy. It's for real! Now imagine that. Those Pleiadians sound like they might be one very interesting group.

I really must consider myself extremely fortunate to have the honor of knowing a Pleiadian personally, and I do hope that I will be able to meet some more of them in the very near future. Although I have read of and heard about some of them already and even know some of their names, I must say I'm still waiting anxiously to be introduced to some more of them. I guess they are still checking me out to see if I can awaken some of the memories from when I knew and befriended them thousands of years ago during my lives as a Hydran. Interestingly enough, I had also befriended the same friend then, as I have now, in this lifetime. I think its safe to say now that our friendship has stood the test of time…another good reason not to doubt my trusty 'contact.'

On the show Star Trek, there is a concept alive called the "prime directive." In real life, there is also a similar concept alive and in use for some, not all of the beings from outer space. They have tried very hard not to interfere in our growth and affairs, but I think a time is coming, very soon, when they will have to violate that same order of noninterference. Personally, I feel that cannot possibly come one moment too soon, for me anyway. Now at this point, I don't really think that I have the physical strength at least to resist any kind of invitation to 'go away' with any desirable bunch of ETs. Unlike my friend years ago, when he was presented with the opportunity to either go with them permanently, or stick around for awhile and try to help some more here on Earth, he bravely chose to stay for awhile longer and do what he could to help to talk to people like me and many others. However, with a little medical attention, perhaps a new back, maybe a new hand, I'm quite sure that anything could be possible, even a change in attitude, on my part. Anyway, I'm glad that he did decide to stay. Perhaps we would never have met if he hadn't and I'd just like to say now, for the record, that I think that it was a very brave and altruistic thing for him to do. I, for one, am eternally grateful to you, you know who you are, for sacrificing this time from your future in order to contact so many different souls and speak with them. I'm quite sure that such selfless patience, generosity, and understanding love cannot, and will not go unnoticed. A caring soul, such as himself and others like him, including Samjese, can only be considered as likely candidates for eternal existence.

Just to expand a little bit on the character of Samjese, she is also Pleiadian, and traveled the distance of some fifty light years from her home world, to ours at such a great speed, that it only took her about 2 weeks to get here; which if you haven't already figured out, is a lot faster than the Elohim can presently travel. I think she probably spent close to 10 years here on and around the Earth before she met with most unfortunate accident. No she's not dead, well, not any more anyway, although she was for a time, but she should be almost completely recovered from her accident now. Let me explain to you just a little more.

You see, she came here with a very clear mission in mind, and has since then become rather famous as she has allowed her craft to be photographed many times, and even to be filmed and recorded on video. But, of course, she doesn't do that for just anybody. No indeed, there was one person selected for her to contact and befriend if possible, and that person was Billy Miers. In order that she would be able to communicate with him comfortably, she spent a lot of the time during her flight to our planet learning to speak his language… or so she thought anyway, as it turned out she had learned the wrong one of two different dialects of the same language. Anyway, with a few adjustments, they were still able to understand each other and communicate, telepathically as well. She learned to speak like him through the use of a kind of hypnotherapy, or some technique that is quite similar anyway, I think most of the time learning was done while she slept, and the craft flew, of course, on 'autopilot.'

I've seen many different pictures of her craft and videos, and even one or two of herself, and I must say, she does look very nice with her long blonde hair and pretty smiling face on. I must also say that I was quite distressed and concerned for her when I found out that she had been injured. It was actually hard to believe that she had been involved in such a ridiculous accident, but I was relieved to find out that she was rescued in time and was going to be all right again, in time. It seems that during one of her clandestine meetings with Billy, that she had become spooked as they sat around a table, talking, when some nosey individual, decided to peek in through the cabin window and get a look at her, or to see what was going on inside. Somehow, during her moment of panic as she tried to beam herself back aboard her ship, she fell or tripped on something and banged her on the table just before she was beamed back into the safety of her "Beam ship."

As she was knocked unconscious by the blow to the head, she lay there on the floor of her craft for several hours before concerned friends of hers discovered her. I think it may even have been Askit, her very close friend that found her lying there in a pool of her own blood. She had technically been dead for some time when they found her, so another race of ETs were contacted by her friends in order that they might help restore life to her body, as they had the knowledge to perform the delicate task of repairing the damage to her head. The name of the group of people that repaired the damage for her is, the Someans, another very advanced race that comes from very far away. Apparently, they filled up the damaged areas of her brain with some kind of synthetic plasma that over time, about 6 months, changes itself into real matter. In this case, brain material. After that, she's been instructed to rest and take it easy back on her home world for as long as it takes, and for a period of about 3 years, she is not to engage in any new thought patterns or challenges until the healing is complete.

It was a long and slow recovery indeed, but entirely necessary for her complete recovery. I'm sure she will be greatly missed in the mean time by some very special people that love her and wish her a perfect future, and those that she loves.

I believe that there are seven major stars in the Pleiades system, called the "seven sisters," that are all occupied by the Pleiadians. However, they don't all live on planets. Some of them, in fact 140,000 of them live on this one particular 'platform' in space. Sort of like what we would call a space station I guess. I've also seen some very beautiful pictures of what these platforms look like and the cities that are on them that they live in, and let me tell you these pictures are not only exciting, but also impressively lovely. The entire plat formed city is covered over with a protective, transparent bubble.

By now I've nearly exhausted my supply of tidbits of information. You know, I had originally hoped that this novel would be at least 300 pages, but it's beginning to look like I'll be lucky to reach a count of 100. Well you know that old saying, about how it is the quality of the subject information that counts, not the quantity of it. Let's hope that holds true for me here. There are still a few items on my agenda though, so I'll get right back into it here, at the risk of sounding like I'm rambling on. I've basically read this and reread this over and over in order to make sure that I haven't left out anything important, and low and behold, there are still several topics that I would like to discuss with you, or should I say, relate to you? Yes, that's it.

So, on that note, I'd just like to tell you about a 'little' battle that I've been made aware of, because I sincerely doubt that any of you have heard of it yet. Now I don't have a whole lot of details or evidence that one can check out to verify my story, but then, this is no court of law either.

This battle happened within the last few decades, probably more like the last two decades. The location, I believe, was somewhere in Europe. It was a battle between four unsuspecting ETs and their craft, and well, by the time it was over, they had fought with 700 – 800 soldiers. It seems that they were taken by surprise while they were landed upon the Earth doing whatever it was they were doing, probably some kind of research. Well obviously they were spotted there in the wilderness, but managed to scramble back to their craft under the protection and cover of their hand lasers. Well they tried to take off, only to discover that their craft had become disabled from flying, so they went on trying to fight for their very lives from the cover of their ship as they were still under constant and relentlessly unprovoked attack.

The battle went on for some hours, and many people died. In fact, most of the 800 soldiers were killed before they managed to kill the ETs. The whole thing seems rather senseless to me. Like I said, the attack upon the ETs was completely unprovoked, not to mention the amount of lives that were wasted, and for what? Certainly not for your entertainment, I'm sure.

I think that it is safe to say that there are more than a few isolated instances of violence between aliens and earthlings. Although, for the most part, any such instance, probably hasn't been, and won't be taken down and recorded in written history. But I know that there has been evidence suggesting that certain areas have been damaged in such a way as to indicate that the damage and destruction caused was done not by the forces of nature, but by some sort of advanced technology.

Just like the ancient ruins that were recently unearthed in India. The ruins were at least 4,000 years old, but for some strange reason, there was a large amount of radioactivity discovered all over the area where the ancient ruins were reaching up out of their own ashen gravesites, as if they were crying out their tragic story of death and destruction. That story is easily deciphered if one pays enough attention to the details. What, if anything could burn everything in its path and leave such a large amount of radiation still lingering? I suppose some kind of laser weapon or further advanced weaponry, like hydrogen or atom bomb or something.

Now these were supposed to have been relatively primitive times, at least in terms of technology and machinery anyway. So therefore we can only conclude that the entire community must have been destroyed by some group of aliens from another planet or galaxy. I just cannot imagine how a technologically insignificant, and basically primitive bunch of peace loving people could possibly be of any threat whatsoever to a race of futuristic people so far away. Certainly they could not possibly be of any military strength to be of any danger to the aliens, so the only way that I could imagine the aliens could feel endangered is through the religious or spiritual beliefs of the natural earthlings. You know, the aliens might have approached the community hoping to subdue them and take them into slavery and a life of devotional service to them. Of course the children of the Earth would not have any of that, so upon their refusal to wait on the typically lazy scavengers, they were promptly executed by their would be 'masters' and an entire city and all the people in it were wiped out…every man, woman, child and animal inclusive.

Of course this left nobody for the aliens to leech off of, or wait on them hand and foot, so they would be forced to move on to other hunting grounds. You know perhaps they weren't so far away after all. I mean, it doesn't make any sense for the aliens to have a skirmish with such a distant neighbor; unless of course, they happened to live much closer to the people on Earth than was originally anticipated. Naturally any display of such advanced technology in weaponry would normally cause one to believe that the perpetrators had come from a far distant galaxy, but only a really close neighbor could possibly have a motive to wipe out an entire community. Perhaps they were only interested in the land occupied by the people, and not the people themselves. Or they may have even been interested in the area directly below the community which leads me to the conclusion that the perpetrators may well have been Satan himself, and his associates, who of course had been living discreetly some kilometers below the Earth's crust.

Just to add a note of completion to the previous story about the battle between the ETs and the soldiers of Earth, I really must say that I was surprised to hear that their ship had been damaged. I guess without the shields activated, as they probably would be with all of the occupants out of the craft that it just may have been possible for something to damage the craft. I neglected to mention earlier that this was done obviously with the use of some kind of heavier artillery than a man could carry. Whether it was done by one of the tanks that was present there, or some kind of air strike from a military aircraft, or even some distant bombardment from heavy duty cannons, it's really hard to say, but nonetheless it is surprising that they managed to disable the ETs craft. I was under the impression that those ships were basically invincible, but again, without shields, they are obviously vulnerable to conventional weapons attack.

OK, time to change the subject again. Or is it? I just had a flash of inspiration for the next line from one of the previous ones. When I was speaking about ships and shields, I thought of their allusion to the body and the soul. I suppose that a body without a soul is a lot like a ship without its shields, and actually, the body is a lot worse off unless of course the individual soul had only temporarily and voluntarily left, only to return again, at will (astral traveling). As in death, if the soul is to leave the body permanently, then naturally the body will die. However, just as in life when a person incurs karmic reactions upon oneself in the physical state, there is also soul karma. Something one cannot escape simply by leaving ones body, as if the act of dearth itself could release you from all of the activities of a lifetime. Of course the actions you perform during a lifetime will have an effect on you after death. In fact, the actions themselves will determine just where you are going after you die and what you will do.

CHAPTER 11

Chosen Ones

Another little detail that I neglected to mention to you was that during the time that Rael spent hanging out with the Elohim and their friends on their planet…well, if you recall, I told you about the DNA machine that has the ability to clone any kind of DNA sample and recreate an exact copy of that same physical being. Well, in fact, just to prove to Rael how effective and efficient the machine is, they made a clone of Rael himself from a sample of his DNA and just to further their point about how amazing the machine actually is, they asked Rael if he carried a picture of his mother. Well, he did have one with him, and from that very same photograph, they managed to recreate an exact duplicate of his very own biological mother simply by feeding the photo into the machine and pressing a few buttons. To his surprise and amazement, out form a doorway in the machine stepped an exactly cloned replica of his mother!

The procedure of cloning people is also the very same method for which any of the good people of this Earth, or chosen children of God, will be restored to life again after their moment of judgment in order that they might live out the rest of their eternal happiness in the kingdom of heaven with their creator.

Now one thought came to mind after reading about that story of Rael being cloned in his book, although nothing like this was mentioned at the time that is that they may have sent Rael's clone back to Earth in order to complete his mission just in case something happened to him. Or they may have felt that he had already earned his chance to stay there with them, and live out the rest of his days of eternal happiness. Again, both of those thoughts are just my own personal ideas that came to mind after reading his book, it's entirely possible that neither of those ideas is true.

Whether it is the original Rael that came back to Earth or the cloned Rael, he seems to be doing a good job of raising the money that is needed for the landing pad, and spreading the message that was given to him, as far as I know, he has managed to complete two books already, maybe more. Once the landing pad is built and the members of the Council of Eternals have arrived, it will be relatively easy for them to communicate with anybody from any country as they have the ability to speak in any language that they desire. I think that little feat is accomplished through the use of some kind of mechanical device that is linked through their ship's computer.

You know, at one point while I was reading Rael's book, they actually said that they would be able to see through Rael's eyes as he journeyed around the world trying to accomplish his mission, raising the necessary funding for the landing pad project. Similarly, they told him not to worry about what to say, that they would somehow tell him how to communicate with people in delicate situations and guide him successfully thought these conversations. They did not however, reveal all the secrets of how these things were done.

As far as the landing pad is concerned, Rael was given very specific instructions how to build it and the adjoining rooms, with exact measurements and dimensions to be followed precisely. Once completed, the actual landing area would be on the roof of the complex, with a hatch that leads from the roof directly into a large meeting room that would actually be the second floor of the structure that is to contain a table of exact measurements, with a certain number of chairs around it that would seat the representatives from the Council of Eternals including Jehovah himself. One thing that they would not tell Rael though is the exact time that they would arrive, if they can be convinced that we the people of Earth are sincere in our desires to welcome them in an amiable way. They are definitely waiting to see our reaction to the announcement that they wish to come here and meet with us!

They are very suspicious and skeptical of how we will receive them, if it will be in a fashion and manner of love and compassion, or if our intentions will not be favorable for them at all. I do hope that they will find favor in our eyes and love in our hearts, and we won't confirm their suspicions of our negativity.

There are a lot more things going on in order to prepare a meeting between ETs and Earthlings. Some of which I do not completely understand, not just because I do not have all of the details, but because of the advanced technology that is being used by them. But one thing that I do understand is that this effort is a very well thought out plan and coordinated effort on the part of more than one separate group of Extraterrestrials from different places and consisting of several different but cooperative races of beings. There is actually a lot more that I would like to tell you about this particular subject, however my good judgment and common sense caution me from revealing too much, too fast. As much as I would like to say more, I am not so sure that it would be a very good idea. I would hate to jeopardize any plans that the IFFW may have for the Imperial Army.

That is not to say, I speculate, that hypothetically a member of the Imperial Army could not have a sudden change of heart, second thoughts about what he or she may be getting themselves into by associating themselves with the 'dark side' unless it is already too late. You know, if the sins of an Imperial agent are not already too great and/ or too many, I would suppose that it would still be possible for that soul to repent from their evil ways and the negative doctrine of the dark Imperial forces.

It's never 'too late' to have a change of heart. I mean, even the most evil soul can be punished, and after the cycle of karma and dharma is complete, what else is left but for the soul to begin again? Obviously some would take longer to learn than others, but what is important, is the end result, as far as reform is concerned. According to Krishna, everyone can be forgiven in the end.

That's a positive thought. I guess it's just a matter of time, and patience for the optimistic amongst you. Unless, you are more active in the peace movement, in which case I suppose then that we would be able to call you an agent of the Federation, of the IFFW. Then I believe that there is a lot more to it than just waiting and hoping, perhaps even praying, and creative visualization. In fact, I am very impressed at the actions that have already been taken, and that's just the steps that I've learned about, which are few in comparison to those I've not yet learned of, I'm sure. Nevertheless, so far, even I, the optimist am surprised and amazed at how much effort is really being put into this thing so far by the grace of the angels that are so diligently applying themselves, on our behalf! And believe me, if it weren't for the efforts of those loving, kind and selfless souls we would most certainly be lost and helpless. I ask you, can you really afford not to be a 'believer'? I can't.

Getting back to the landing pad and all its exact specifications for just a moment, although there is a precise number of seats to be included, and they have indicated that these seats will be for meeting with our worldly 'leaders' or heads of Government, they weren't really specific about just who they want to meet with them. Well, whoever they will be, you can be sure that they are quite serious about getting right down to business as the closeness of the landing sight to the meeting room would indicate. I suppose that it's not all going to be super serious negotiations though, because of the onsite swimming pool there, it seems there will also be time for relaxation as well.

I think perhaps the reason that they didn't tell Rael the exact time of their arrival is because they are just being cautious and thinking ahead. They have been very careful not to tell Rael any more than he absolutely needs to know so that in the case that he might be captured and tortured, or made to talk another way, perhaps with drugs or whatever, he won't be able to betray their confidence even if he wanted to. You know, the less that he knows, the less likely he is to get into some kind of dangerous situation.

Unfortunately that very same rule applies not only to Rael, but to me as well, and probably everybody else as well. It's a pretty good general rule of thumb that can be effectively applied to any situation, and in most cases, it will benefit the person.

However, if you happen to be close enough to somebody important, but still not know some of their deepest secrets, that usually means that you might still know enough to be a prime candidate for questioning.

Now there is still a little bit of information that I would like to share with those of you who don't already know about it. And so, although I believe that the Government of the United States is doing their very best to keep this a secret from y'all, I just have to let the cat out of the bag in this case, much to their displeasure I'm sure. There has been a lot of sightings and UFO activity around the area of Arizona and New Mexico, especially near a place called Dulce, New Mexico. Well that is far from just a coincidence; in fact there is a very good reason for all of that activity. The reason is that there is a secret underground facility located near Dulce that is part of an Alien Government alliance. In fact, that is also the reason that there have been numerous cattle mutilations as well in that very same area. I've already explained why the mutilations are occurring, but now you may come to understand why they have perhaps been happening a little more often in that particular area.

Within that same underground complex there does exist 7 stories of a building only the floors are counted from 1 to 7 not upwards into the sky as you might suspect a building would be, but as you go from the first floor to the second and onwards to the 7th, you will find that you are actually going deeper and deeper into the Earth, so that by the time you've reached the 7th level, you would be at the deepest level underground. As well, with every floor that you descend, and with each and every change of the numerical level, there is also a change of classification. That is to say that with every floor you descend, you must have one step higher of clearance for access to Government secrets.

Apparently each floor is full of little rooms and cages where people and animals are kept for experiments. Of course every corridor is monitored carefully and the entire complex is very heavily guarded; only those with special clearance levels of different classifications are allowed to go into the place.

Once you've managed to be unlucky enough to get yourself captured or abducted by these people, and if they take you there, there is very little chance that you will ever see the light of day again; there really is no escape! I'll tell you now, just in case you haven't figured it out yet, that is one very scary place and I hope and pray that they never decide that I should become one of their permanent residents. Although I do believe highly in my guardian angel(s), I really see no need to put them to the test. My faith is strong and true. So on that note, I feel like there has been enough said about Dulce, New Mexico. Do not get me wrong however, that is the chance that I feel is worth taking in order to keep the good people of this earth informed about what is actually and really going on all around us here.

We have the right to know and be informed about anything that may affect our loved ones and us. Once that right is taken away, well, then you really can't blame anyone for what happens next as a result of the consequences of such suppression of the truth, and I can think of a few more tasty words that might well describe the actions of those kinds of individuals and organizations. However, I won't get into that name calling business too much, and let your imagination be free to think whatever it will about all this.

If you think that underground complex that I told you about is surprising, then you'll certainly find this next bit of information even more so, perhaps even unbelievable. And if there is anything that I can say to upset anyone who might be considered a friend of a M.I.B, this next secret of theirs might well be the thing to reveal to you.

And so I will insert a copy of the map of all the hidden underground and up till now, secret interconnected web of tunnels and other complexes used by a race of aliens and humans who seem to have nothing but contempt for all who are not like them in mind and intention. And if anyone should stumble upon the entrance to any one of these underground hideouts during a carefree romp through the countryside, then that person would probably be shot or captured by the guards (or government agents) stationed at every entrance and around the perimeter of their secret complexes.

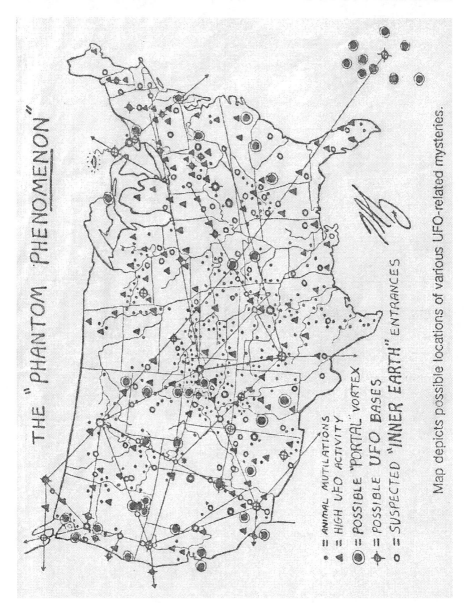

THE "PHANTOM PHENOMENON"

• = ANIMAL MUTILATIONS
▲ = HIGH UFO ACTIVITY
◉ = POSSIBLE "PORTAL" VORTEX
✦ = POSSIBLE UFO BASES
○ = SUSPECTED "INNER EARTH" ENTRANCES

Map depicts possible locations of various UFO-related mysteries.

I think that it is quite safe to say that one of these races of aliens that finds itself in alliance with our government(s) of this earth, is the group that we call the grays. I think that it is also safe to say that the grays themselves may well be associated with Satan and his buddies. You know the ones Buzz stumbled upon in their underground lair? Further, these are the people (and co.) that I believe are trying to make friends with a certain well know author (unlike myself) who is unwittingly falling right into their web. The person that I am referring to here is the one, the only, Whitley Strieber, author of "Communion".

My message to him is, be careful, don't get too curious too fast about the strange visits that you had once upon a time. You just might regret where you could end up. He might even find himself in a cage on one of those seven underground levels that I mentioned before. According to an ex guard/government agent who once worked there, stationed during the time he was enlisted into military service, he says that the further down that he went, although his clearance was limited to less than the highest which would have given him access to the last level, he could see that certain 'little grey aliens" were involved and appeared to be quite free to roam around the complex entering into it on any level that they desired. Somehow I don't think many/any civilians(s) could obtain even the first level of clearance necessary to enter into and freely leave such a secret complex.

CHAPTER 12

Silver Bullets

Out of this entire adventure that you all have so graciously entered into with me, this next part seems to me to be the saddest part of all of it so far. However, it is also a very necessary part as well, and so therefore, unfortunately, I must accept the inevitable and somehow wind this whole story up into what we have come to know just such an occasion as the conclusion to the story.

Now I know that I have not covered all of the territory that I may have wanted to, and there are still some secrets that I could probably go into, but for various reasons, I've decided that the time for that is not quite ripe yet, and so therefore, again unfortunately, this has resulted in a much shorter story than I had originally planned. Oh well, I'm sure you have all heard of that old saying about how it is the quality of the information that really counts, and not the quantity…I only hope that saying will be found to be true in this particular case. Another positive way to view this is to consider the fact that most of this information that I have been sharing with you all is, well, maybe not all of it would be considered 'positive' but it certainly does seem to be necessary nevertheless, and so therefore, I truly hope that all of this more than just appears to me to be helpful, but I wish that at least some of this information will really be helpful to at least some of you, and if it has been in any way useful to even one of you, then I hope it should continue to inspire you and help you in some small way, even if it may only serve to deliver you some peace of mind and spirit.

Finally, we can only take it as a good sign that, seeing as how my message has been one of perhaps sometimes painful revelations, that it is a good thing after all that the whole thing has not become ominously long and drawn out and perhaps even boring. I would hate to lose my audience just because the message was far too cumbersome, negative, or uninteresting.

Somehow it just seems too easy to leave off with this altogether too short and sweet, and so just to fill it out a bit and round it off some, I'm going to mention briefly a subject which would be better off if it were merely folklore, or fairytale and not true at all in any way, whatsoever. Perhaps because this is a scary topic, and really frightening concept, it is just as well that I won't be able to dwell upon it for that long.

There is another reason that I don't particularly want to go into absolutely every detail that I've come across in my journey, and that is simply because of the fact that I really do feel that it is important to convince those that I can of the authenticity of the things that I have said to you. If I were to tell you everything I know about this subject, I'm quite sure that some of the information that I've related to you would be unbelievable and might well just cast a shadow of suspicion upon some of the very important and true circumstances that we have covered here in this book. You know, if even just one thing I were to tell you were absolutely unbelievable to you, there is a great chance that one might not also find some of the other information just as unbelievable.

Just to prove my point, I'm going to risk my reputation and credibility and give to you a perfect example of exactly what I'm talking about. How many of you have heard of the old werewolf story? You know...full moon, ferocious appetites, and silver bullets? Now how many of you actually think that there might be a possibility that there is even an ounce of truth to any of this? I really have no idea what the ratio of percentages of believers to nonbelievers is, but I would bet one of my silver bullets that most of you do not believe that monsters such as werewolves have ever really existed. Which is perhaps just as well, for the less we believe in them, the harder it is for them to actually exist, especially in our minds. But in this very real world, I've been told that werewolves really have existed on this planet, and in fact, could only be killed with a silver projectile!

Now I'm not even sure that I can believe there is any truth to that statement and even if I could bring myself to accept such a claim, I'm not so sure that I could admit to believing such a thing. Although I can't imagine why, I've believed in far crazier concepts I'm sure. I really have no reason to doubt my source; I guess it is just another one of those things that one would like to see with one's own eyes before committing to belief.

Anyway that's all I had to say about that subject, and I hope that I have made my point clear about credibility and all that; if indeed there is any clarity at all to be found in this subject. You know a lot of the things that I have told to you all have been laughed at and ridiculed by more than one, but for all of it, the hecklers just can't seem to convince me otherwise, and certainly, the mocking of a few 'know-it-alls' do not in any way disprove any of the things I have said, and anyway, their laughter only makes me realize that their opinions no longer interest me at all.

Anyway, if you can believe that werewolves really do exist, then you can believe in almost anything, which is why you've made it to the end of this book. However, I realize that in no way implies with any great certainty that each and every one of you that has made it this far through my story believes each and every little thing that I've told you here, but it's a safe bet that most of you do feel that some of this could quite likely be reality, and are not that surprised either. In fact, some of you may even be finding that some of your suspicions are now being confirmed, and therefore may even be feeling a little relieved, just to know that your intuitions are still in fact, just as sharp as they ever were, but perhaps not as sharp as they will be?

And so, it is with great sadness, mixed with a great sense of joy of completion, that I must really try and bring this all to a tidy end. Although, somehow I feel that once I've actually finished this and sent it off to a publisher that I think I'll probably remember a hundred things that I wanted to talk about.

But I do have other projects that I must get on with…specifically a Sonata that I composed has to be recorded and sent off to a publisher as well, and then the slate will be cleared for other projects and new ideas. I must say thank you for being so curious as to follow your heart and trust the path that it takes you on, even in the face of opposition and false ridicule. If you always travel this way…your paths will be many and interesting as well as exciting. May you find this to be true (and all will love you and yours).

I'd like to leave you all with a multiple choice question before I say goodbye, and add that the answer to the question can be found by following the trusty trail of the heart:

Who built the pyramids?

a. The Egyptians and their slaves

b. The Atlantians

c. Extra-Terrestrials

d. One or more of the above

Or, if you prefer,

*Which of the above are **not** responsible for the construction of the pyramids?*

a. None of them

b. All of them

c. The Stone Masons

d. Aliens

Now I'm having so much fun that I just can't seem to bring this whole thing to an end. So instead of tapping my enormously vivid imagination in order to fill up some space and make this drag on forever, I'm going to include a map of the known universe, at least what has been charted so far. I'm sure that there is a lot more space out there to discover and map.

But that's hardly enough to fill up and occupy the space of your eager and spongy minds now is it? So, on that note, I think that we should do a slight review of the material that we have covered so far, so I'm going to ask you all…out of all of the information that I've related to you, which of it do you think is the most important, or might be the most likely to have any influence or effect on your life, either directly or indirectly?

Now that I've asked you all a question, I just can't resist answering the question myself. For me anyway, it is difficult to say just what might be slightly more important or relevant, compared to any other little tidbit, but if I had to guess out of all that I have written, I would have to say, that the threat, or fear, of evil aliens, Satan, and our own "God" combined don't match the thought of that huge solar giant speeding toward our galaxy at unimaginable speeds, it is the scariest of all, and quite likely will have the most direct effect, and certainly, it throws a wrench into the future plan for all of us here on Earth, not just some of us, but all of us will be affected by that, if indeed the source of this information is reliable and the prediction is true, which it just may be. I don't know, but that just seems to be the most shocking of all of the information, that and the Grays walking through walls to kidnap and drug and enslave us poor defenseless humans.

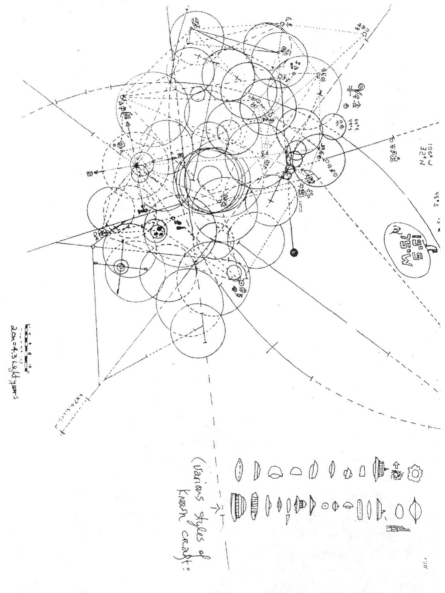

One other interesting point that just seems to scream out at me from the page that it is written upon is that here we have, if we believe, an invitation from "God" into heaven, without having to die to get there and if you've managed to get that far, an invitation to eternal life is sure to follow. Think of the possibilities that the landing pad would bring with it. Should we decide to allow it here on Earth? What "God" is really offering us, is a chance to get to know him, and maybe even get along with him and his associates, and even learn to become friends with them!

Just think what that would mean, thousands of years of prophecy could be changed in an instant. Satan and the "Imperial" army could be spared and the future could be bright for all of us! Could that really be? Who dares to fly in the face of well-known, long established prophecy? Surely the soul that dares to do that or even dares to mention to conceive of such a radical deed is the soul of a Creator. It could indeed be said that KRSNA lives in the heart of that person, and in the Soul of that soul. Surely that individual can look forward to forgiveness and perhaps even a brighter and warmer Nirvana. Who knows? I think it not impossible, that the great and powerful Holy Spirit left room in the story that it wrote, so that even you may write a story in the chapters, and learn to be creative, perhaps change the course of accepted future, for the better I'm sure...such an addition can only improve on an already good thing, I'm sure!

So I guess by now that your all wondering how that movie way back near page #1 is coming along, eh? Well this is a book, not a movie, and if I tell you how it turns out, won't that only spoil the ending for you? Yes, I think that it probably would just ruin the rest of the movie for y'all, so I've decided that it would be better if I let y'all just wait until you can see the movie for yourselves. Perhaps I shouldn't have even brought it up. But I must admit, I'm a little curious myself. I guess I'll just have to wait patiently.

So it must be getting very obvious that I've really come to a big empty space in my mind where there is nothing left to say. Not a lot unlike the map of the universe that I showed you a few pages age. There are some scribbles in the center of it all, with a lot of space of the outside around the edges, and it all looks slightly impressive, perhaps almost like something that one could believe in, perhaps with just a little confirmation, it could look just like the truth. Only if you were to ask me exactly how to decipher that map, I'm sure that I would say something like...

"You'll just have to use your imagination and natural, God given intelligence because that's all that I have to go on."

"Al....Al....Alpha!"

"What? What happened?" I asked, leaping back into an awake and conscious state, spilling a bowl of popcorn off of my lap where it had been nestled comfortably as I dozed. Looking over at the kids I could see that they were both dead to the world (asleep), Sand with his head resting on Colour's shoulder, and Colour resting her head upon his.

"They slept through the whole movie!" I exclaimed, looking back at my wife as if she might have some sort of explanation that could satisfy my sudden sense of disappointment at their lack of interest.

"We all fell asleep at some point during the movie...including you Al." As she kneeled down to pick up the mess of popcorn that I'd created, she added, "I must admit, I'm guilty as well, the only reason that I'm awake now my dear, is because of your thunderous snoring."

"I thought that painful operation cured me from my snoring problem."

"Well, it didn't," she said, "but you've definitely ceased to do it as much as you did before the operation."

"Well," I said, getting up to help her clean up the mess, "maybe we can all have another look at it tomorrow evening?"

"Um I ahh... wonder if maybe we should wait until they are a little bit older. Then maybe they'll be able to understand it a little more. Not to mention being able to stay awake later."

THE END?

EPILOGUE:

Predictions And Revelations

Remember in the first chapter when the little girl asks the question, "where did it all begin?" Well that question is not only the inspiration for this novella, but it is the theme behind it all. As a young man I had many questions about life and its origins, and I resolved to go out and find the answers even if it took me my whole life. Believe me it nearly has and may yet. However the important thing is that I think I've found all those answers or most of them anyway. This novella is the culmination of thirty years of research and writing. The main thing that I am trying to do here is share the information that I uncovered with others that may have wondered as I have. For the most part, I'm passing on these answers as they came to me, and in some cases exactly as I got them. Those instances should be obvious to you. I haven't gone too deeply into what I think or feel about all of this or how it connects and relates to other spiritual teachings except where I felt it was necessary. Am I the only one to notice that there seems to be a separation and even conflict between the physical and the spiritual religious teachings? That is the one thing that has been bothering me throughout this entire project. How can the ELO-HIM being the creators that they are possibly say and believe that there is no spirit? They think that life is only physical and when we die, that's it, there is nothing more! We all know there is more to it than that. The Gita teaches that the individual soul is attached to the physical body at the third chakra and the Super-soul lies in the heart. The Gita also tells us about Yama-Raja, the lord of death that decides what is to come for us after we die, according to our earthly deeds. I am convinced that Jehovah, the president of the Council of Eternals is that same being. I'm not so sure that he knows it but I think whoever left him the time capsule with the DNA information was probably his creator. I wonder if he has ever had such a thought. If it is true than that would make the Great Spirit ... the Holy Ghost ... KRSNA his father\creator and they need to talk.

This was meant to be only a few short pages about predictions etc., however I can see that it is going to be a little bit more than that. So this brings me to Jesus. Most of us will agree that he was here some 2,000 years ago and was crucified and resurrected. Now we have learned how it was possible for the ELO-HIM to beam up his body and clone it. What about his soul? Obviously he would have the option of entering back into the body of his cloned self or remaining a free spirit, which would necessitate allowing another soul to occupy it. It is my theory that the latter is probably true. I say that because I've read and heard too many stories and accounts of near death experiences, and channeled after-life experiences about people/souls meeting Jesus in the spiritual realm. Most recently I've heard about an Indian who was very sick and traveled to that world and met Jesus and came back with a message of peace and love and prophecies of the white men almost taking away the way of life of the Indians before they regained it. That happened in the 1800's and has since been proven true. Another touching account I read about was a man who had a vision of John Lennon and went on to channel him and was told how he met with Jesus after he was shot and died and traveled through the tunnel of light and met his mother who showed him around. If you want to read more about these two stories as well as some interesting stuff about the Sasquatch, see "Strange Northwest" by Chris Bader and Hancock House publishers page 123. When I read or hear these stories, they just seem to ring true. Somehow I feel inside the story teller is sincere and believes what they are saying is the truth, and that faith is transferred over to the open hearted and minded listener so you say to yourself, "yeah that seems like it could be just so." What about the friendly white light being that people meet during their near death experiences who shows them the 'movie' of their life and makes them feel how they should about the things that they did wrong in their lives? This being shows all this within moments, what took a lifetime to live is summed up in seconds. Who or what is that? Is this being Jesus or is it the Holy Ghost? Obviously we as spiritual beings have a responsibility to inform those that come from the sky that we may well have something to teach them. After all every one thousand years they just clone themselves and jump into their new body, so they would have no first hand experience in that spiritual world, or of reincarnation, or of any of the marvelous things that a free spirit encounters throughout it's travels.

Perhaps their Jesus doesn't dwell in the body they cloned for him; after all he did curse his father upon the cross did he not? He suffered greatly and may have decided to just stay out of his body and remain in the spiritual realm, whenever he died, where there would have certainly been others there to assist him and make him feel welcome and perhaps exorcise his curiosity a little bit. Now things seem to be falling into place and making a bit more sense, to me anyway. I wish the same could happen to the world we live in. The world of business and economics can be so cold and un-loving with the rich getting richer and the poor getting poorer. If it were up to me, if I was the king of the Universe, I would give everybody a million dollars just for being born into this world. We could just print the money, its value could be based on the natural resources of wealth that are already here in the Earth like gold and silver etc. and just by leaving some of it buried, well it would be considered safe, like as if it was in a vault. I seriously doubt that it would be the first time that money was created simply by printing it. Have you ever wondered where the governments of Earth get their trillions of dollars? Have you ever tried to do the math? What the average person makes in a year and pays into taxes, it just does not seem to add up to the amount that they are spending. Why do they continue to spend so much on making war with our brothers and sisters? We could so easily feed everyone on the planet and make comfortable housing for all. People could stand up and be happy healthy members of society. With the million dollars that we get just for being born, not to be-little the birthing process, I'm sure that most of us would make a go of it and invest the money into something creative that we love to do, make a sustainable business, feel successful in life and never have to worry about our next meal or how we will pay the rent. Of course the skeptics would argue that it would never work because people would just squander their wealth or for some other reason, blah blah blah ... but let's be honest, it would not hurt to try. How else would we ever know for sure who was right, the negatives or the positives?

Okay, it's time for me to go even further out onto the limb and pass on to you a prediction as it was revealed to me by my Pleiadian contact. Everyone must have heard of the New World Order, (N.W.O.), at this stage in the game, if not then you surely have now. It is to consist of all of North American and South American states under one flag, one government ... the N.W.O. On their flag will be the symbol of the eagle. After they have ruled for a time, then another entity will arise out of Italy calling itself the phoenix. This one will try to take over the whole world, and it's my understanding that he won't be real nice about it. However, there is hope on the horizon for those of us that will endure thus far. The end of the phoenix will signal the time that we are all waiting for, the time of the Angels. Then we will see the return of Jesus and all the angels and the Inter-galactic Federation of the Free Worlds. I truly hope that I live to see all this come to pass, and not just because it would be embarrassing to falsely predict a prophecy.

I know people worry about losing their culture and heritage, even their languages. I have those feelings too, I'd like to speak Sanskrit or Icelandic or Gaelic, all part of my personal heritage. The one thing that we all have in common though is that we are all considered simply human. Surely there must come a time when we can all communicate with each other ... all races from all galaxies. You remember I told you of an inter-galactic peace treaty and the common language of the E.T.'s? Well that is the beginning of it all and I say that it is a good thing. I consider myself an eternal optimist and will always be un-afraid of change for the better of us all. Let us not fear the N.W.O. or the phoenix, let us keep up the faith and love each other, unconditionally if possible, and we'll get through it all and soon be re-united with our space brothers and sisters, and our Creators. The Gita says that all life begins and ends in space. I know life can be tough, believe me, I've not been raised on any silver spoon, but if we continue to love and believe and stand up for what is right, (you'll know, you'll feel it in your heart), then we will over-come all the difficulties and make it through, shining. Those of you born into more fortunate lives should not be afraid to make a difference in the world, your world, help those that you can, set a good example for the governments.

I know that some of you already are doing some amazing things and I urge you to continue if possible, I'm so very proud of you for trying and love you for it and wish y'all a perfect future. Those of you in darker circles, come into the light. It is not yet too late to save your self and your soul. Don't think for one minute, oh I'll just die and hide my soul and reincarnate later. Believe me, there is no hiding from the Paramatma. He will find you and show you how easy it is for the one that knows everything to hide your soul for you, perhaps by stretching a buffalo skin over it, or some other appropriate animal skin, yeah He may let you hide in the animal kingdom for a very long time. Would you really like that? Perhaps you might just remain out of the physical world forever separated from those you love. Where will you be then?

Okay, I've been saving this revelation for the end, just because I was hesitant to mention it at all out of concern for my health and safety and those that are close to me. Not to mention the very life of this book itself. Sometimes people take offense at being exposed, but I've said enough in defense of the government, they still have time to change and let's face it; I'm not the first to speak out about government atrocities. In the past many people have spoken up about things that are wrong and I feel better for it and thank them. I was going to go into the whole 9/11 thing but there is already enough evidence to prove that it was indeed an inside job and that would take up too much of my time and space right now. If that sounds like a lame excuse, that may just be too quick of a judgment. It really is a huge subject and even though I don't think I'm an expert on it, I have seen convincing evidence, or lack of evidence, to convince me the United States government is lying about all of it. By lack of evidence I refer to the fact that no bodies or plane parts were recovered from Pennsylvania, no plane parts were found at the Pentagon, no wing holes could be seen in the side of the building and again no plane parts. In the slow motion footage of the towers falling you can clearly see explosions going off all the way down, and many witnesses including the fire fighters say they heard such explosions ... you can even see a bright white flash of light just prior to the plane and its shadow touching the building. Why did they discover truckloads of gold halfway between towers four and five as if trying to escape before it was too late? Did you hear about the German computer specialists that found evidence of insider trading on 32 of the mainframes that were recovered from the damage? Those people knew something was about to go down and felt safe enough that their trading evidence would be destroyed. The Germans handed the evidence over to the F.B.1. but nothing has ever come of it. Yes there is lot's more like that for those of you who are not afraid to look for the truth. There are horrible things that they do with your tax dollars, which brings me to the point I was getting to.

My source tells me that the C.I.A. and the heads of the M.I.B created many of our common diseases in a laboratory. Diseases like aids; hepatitis, sars, mad cow disease, and bird flu all have been engineered by the bad guys. Simply traveling to a foreign country, like China, and going into a restaurant and ordering an expensive meal introduced one of these diseases. So imagine if you will, a couple of M.I.B.'s sitting there enjoying a choice cut of meat, carrying on like a couple of genuine tourists would, perhaps flashing around their cash and leaving large tips so that they would seem like high rollers. Well, they have finished all the expensive wine but not eaten all of their dinner. Carefully they plop a briefcase on the table and open it in such a way so as to block anyone from seeing what they are really doing behind it. Now with the cover they have created they reach inside the case and pull out a vial and a brush and apply the amount of virus that they need to a remaining piece of meat. Then some hungry chef who doesn't want to waste the meal either eats it himself or puts it into the stew for some unlucky customers, and viola ... the deadly disease is introduced into the human race. Do you see how your government spends your hard earned tax dollars? Can you humble yourselves enough to face and accept the truth?

The beauty of Mad Cow disease for the government is that not only do they get to make people sick, which they profit from, but suddenly people are forced to buy only local beef, which they also profit from. That action also gives them more bargaining power when they want to convince us all that free trade is a good thing. I know some of you won't believe that they could go to such lengths to make us sick, but you really must question their motives for irradiating food. At some point, surely everyone will begin to wonder why an advanced civilized world has so many 'uncontrollable' diseases. Some of us believe that there is a cure for every disease growing in the earth around us; we just need to discover the particular plant, root, or herbal flower. Take for instance wheat grass, it is said that it can cure even lethal doses of cancer, yet nobody in power seems interested in it. It upsets me when I think of how much money is spent on cancer research yet nobody wants to acknowledge one of the main sources. When I try to talk to people about this, they often scoff at the idea of food irradiation, yet it remains a very real concern. I do have a book that is the minutes of the meeting of the standing committee on the subject of labeling food that is irradiated. It goes a long way in helping to convince people that it is real so I will include a couple of pages that I copied for you in case you want a copy for yourself. Once you see the House of Commons seal on it you may be more inclined to believe. (See following page). I remember about the same time that the report came out we in the health food community where petitioning them in order to stop them from getting into the organic food stores and spreading this radiation around. Thank God we where successful, but how long can we keep them at bay? Now twenty years have passed and still no action has been taken to label such foods. How many of us have gotten sick and even died not knowing that our own government is to blame? I can tell immediately when I've eaten something that has been irradiated by the burning sensation in my stomach. Surely you have felt that and wondered if it is just acid re-flux or bad digestion? You know the Gita says that if someone poisons you it is a crime worthy of the punishment of instant death. That comes to me as no surprise since it also says that the stomach is the center of pleasure.

Speaking of poison, would you believe that the present day flu vaccine contains a small amount of mercury? I know that a lot of you won't want to believe it but it is indeed part of the government's plan to keep us sick and keep our numbers from becoming too great. This is just one of the ways that they can give you a chemical lobotomy. If you really want to find out more about this subject and other related material, just have a look at the movie "End Game", by Alex Jones. As a further note, the only remedy that I am aware of for removing heavy metals from the body is to ingest organic flax seed oil, the kind with the seed skins, or shells still on it. They call that kind of oil "high lignon" because of the remaining skins.

Now it should come as no great surprise to you that the government also wants to make all of our natural God given herbs that are presently available to us in any health food store, or growing around us in the earth, available only through a prescription method. That would make it very difficult to enjoy a simple cup of herbal tea. I guess that won't matter much if and when the Koreans decide to invade us here in North America like my Pleiadian friend has warned me about. This information is beginning to depress me a little so I am going to hope and pray for the time of the Angels and our subsequent rescue from the evil governments of the Earth to come as soon as possible. In the meantime I can only hope that we can come together as one and teach these people a better way. Somehow I think that only divine intervention is going to do the trick though. In God we trust. In our hearts we love. And, perhaps if our souls are as one as we pray together, then the Star People will trust us and let their hearts be moved into believing that we really do want them to come to Earth, openly, and without any fear of being attacked.

So keep on believing my brothers and sisters, keep on praying to give them strength and love and let them know that we are sincerely desiring the assistance of the IFFW.

HOUSE OF COMMONS
CANADA

Food Irradiation

REPORT OF THE STANDING COMMITTEE ON CONSUMER AND
CORPORATE AFFAIRS ON THE QUESTION OF FOOD IRRADIATION
AND THE LABELLING OF IRRADIATED FOODS

MARY COLLINS, M.P.
CHAIRPERSON

MAY 1987

Recommended Labelling Format — Irradiated Ingredients

Sample label:

INGREDIENTS: CHICKEN,
POTATOES, CARROTS, ONIONS,
FLOUR, PALM OIL, MILK
POWDER, SUGAR, SALT,
SPICES.

IRRADIATED

minimum size 4.8 millimeters
(3/16 inch)

POTATOES, ONIONS, FLOUR,
SPICES

otherwise, same size as labelling
requirements prescribed by Section 14
of the Consumer Packaging and
Labelling Regulations

As noted all irradiated ingredients must be listed separately under the word
"IRRADIATED" accompanied by the symbol. Other specifications are outlined in
Recommendations 17 and 18.

CHAPTER 2

The Labelling of Irradiated Foods

(i)   Form of Labelling

The Standing Committee believes that the right to be informed about the nature and quality of food and to exercise meaningful choices when selecting food products is of prime importance to consumers. This becomes particularly significant as public concern about the safety of food products grows and as evidence of the harmful effects of substances that were once thought to be safe comes to light. Labelling food ingredients is one method of providing information to consumers so that informed choices can be made.

The labelling of irradiated foods may be seen by some as an adjunct to the proposal to classify food irradiation as a food process. Labelling, however, should be viewed as a matter which is distinct from the regulatory status of food irradiation. As irradiation is now permitted for a selected number of food items, labelling requirements for these uses should be addressed irrespective of potential future applications.

Since the *Food and Drug Regulations* define "any source of radiation" as a food additive, irradiated foods must be labelled. The current regulations respecting the labelling of irradiated flour and whole wheat flour require that where these products have been treated with gamma radiation from a Cobalt-60 source, the label must carry a statement to the effect that they have been processed or treated with ionizing radiation. No labelling format, however, is indicated. The labels of irradiated spices, potatoes, onions and wheat must also indicate that these products have been irradiated, but again there would appear to be no standard format for such labelling. As well, imported irradiated foods must be limited to those specified in the existing regulations and labelled accordingly.

Classifying irradiation as a food additive ensures that foods treated with ionizing radiation will be labelled. Classifying it as a process, however, eliminates the mandatory labelling requirements. At present, some food processes require labelling to indicate their use while others do not. For example, foods which are canned or frozen are not labelled to indicate these processing methods — the use of either being evident from the nature of the container or the product. On the other hand, pasteurization, a process the use of which is not evident to consumers of milk, is indicated on the label of milk containers. Food irradiation is analogous to pasteurization in that the consumer has no tangible means of determining whether a food has been irradiated. In the

BASIC SUMMARY:

An informative in-depth look at the lives of several E.T.'s and aliens, what their lives are like on their planets in their galaxies, what their crafts (spaceships) are like, and how they are connected to us here on Earth. As well, how they are important in our religion and military strength. This novel also looks at some historical revelations, future predictions and current happenings including an interesting collection of anecdotes regarding an ex-C.I.A. agent who gets his wishes granted. These are some things that the author thinks everyone needs to know about God, the devil and U.F.O.s. This book has been a long time in the making, (20 years), but somehow it still manages to remain ahead of it's time...in most cases. It is my sincere desire to share this with as many people as I possibly can so that they may make an informed decision about their future. I thank you for you're interest and wish y'all and those that you love a perfect future.